"Aiden?"

The sudden silence must have become too much for her, because Christina moved forward as if to continue down the stairs.

The polite thing would have been to step aside, but the ache to feel that body against his once more kept him perversely still. She slowed within a hair's breadth, tension mounting once more. "Aiden?"

"So you're really willing to do this?" he asked, almost holding his breath as he awaited her answer. What delicious torture to spend the next year with this woman and keep his hands to himself. Could he? *This was a huge mistake.*

"I don't know. I don't think I can, you know, share a bed with you."

The way her voice trailed off told him how very uncomfortable she was, which only awakened images of making her very comfortable in a bed for two.

Maybe he could find a way to make this work.

* * *

A Bride's Tangled Vows is part of the
Mill Town Millionaires series.

* * *

If you're on Twitter,
tell us what you think of Harlequin Desire!
#harlequindesire

Dear Reader,

I'm so excited to bring you the first in my Mill Town Millionaires series, *A Bride's Tangled Vows,* because it lets me share with you a country and culture that I love. Christina is the quintessential Southern heroine—soft when she wants to be, strong when she needs to be. And she's the perfect match for hardheaded prodigal grandson Aiden Blackstone (even if he fights it every step of the way).

Springtime in the southern U.S. is a unique time of turbulent weather that leads to new beginnings. Much like life in Blackstone Manor. I hope you find all that and more in this series.

As always, I love to hear from my readers. Please visit my website at www.daniwade.com or follow me on Facebook or Twitter to let me know if you enjoyed this romance with Southern flair!

Dani

A BRIDE'S TANGLED VOWS

DANI WADE

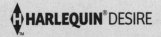

Recycling programs
for this product may
not exist in your area.

ISBN-13: 978-0-373-73335-4

A BRIDE'S TANGLED VOWS

Copyright © 2014 by Katherine Worsham

Printed in U.S.A.

Dani Wade

astonished her local librarians as a teenager when she carried home ten books every week—and actually read them all. Now she writes her own characters, who clamor for attention in the midst of the chaos that is her life. Residing in the southern United States with a husband, two kids, two dogs and one grumpy cat, she stays busy until she can closet herself away with her characters once more.

To the late Beverly Barton—you gave freely of your encouragement and advice the first time you read this story, and told me one day my time would come. Now that it's here, I wish I could share it with you. But I know your gorgeous smile is lighting up heaven. I look forward to seeing you again....

One

Aiden Blackstone suppressed a shiver that had nothing to do with the afternoon thunderstorm raging all around him. For a moment, he remained immobile, staring at the elaborate scrolls carved into the heavy oak door before him. A door he'd promised himself he'd never pass through again—at least, not while his grandfather was alive.

I should have come back here, Mother, only to see you.

But he'd sworn never to let himself be locked inside the walls of Blackstone Manor again. He'd thought he had all the time he would need to make his absence up to his mother. In his youthful ignorance, he hadn't realized everything he'd be giving up to uphold his vow. Now he was back to honor another vow—a promise to see that his mother was taken care of.

The thought had his stomach roiling. Shaking it off, he reached for the old-fashioned iron knocker shaped like a bear's head. The cab had already left. On a day plagued by steamy, ferocious southern thunderstorms, he certainly wouldn't be walking the ten miles back to Black Hills, no matter how much he dreaded this visit. His nausea eased as he reminded himself that he wouldn't be here for long—only as long as necessary.

Knocking again, he listened intently for footsteps on the other side of the door. *It wasn't really home if you had to wait for someone to answer.* He'd walked away with the surety that only comes with untried youth. Now he returned a different man, a success on his own terms. He just wouldn't have the satisfaction of rubbing his grandfather's nose in it.

Because James Blackstone was dead.

The knob rattled, then the door swung inward with a deep creak. A tall man, his posture still strong despite the gray hair disappearing from his head, blinked several times as if not sure his aging eyes were trustworthy. Though he'd left his childhood home on his eighteenth birthday, Aiden recognized Nolen, the family butler.

"Ah, Master Aiden, we've been expecting you," the older man said.

"Thank you," Aiden returned with polite sincerity, stepping closer to look into the butler's faded blue eyes. Lightning cracked nearby and thunder almost immediately boomed with wall-rattling force, the storm a reflection of the upheaval deep in Aiden's core.

Still studying his face, the older man opened the door wide enough for Aiden and his luggage. "Of course," Nolen said, shutting out the pouring rain behind them. "It's been a long time, Master Aiden."

Aiden searched the other man's voice for condemnation, but found none. "Please leave your luggage here. I'll take it up once Marie has your room ready," Nolen instructed.

So the same housekeeper—the one who'd baked cookies for him and his brothers while they were grieving the loss of their father—was still here, too. They said nothing ever changed in small towns. They were right.

Aiden swept a quick glance around the open foyer, finding it the same as when he'd left, too. The only anomaly was an absent portrait that captured a long-ago moment in time—his parents, himself at about fifteen and his younger twin brothers about a year before his father's death.

Setting down his duffel and laptop case and shaking

off the last drops of rain, he followed Nolen's silent steps through the shadowy breezeway at the center of the house. The gallery, his mother had always called this space that opened around the central staircase. It granted visitors an unobstructed view of the elaborate rails and landings of the two upper floors. Before air-conditioning, the space had allowed a breeze through the house on hot, humid, South Carolina afternoons. Today the sounds of his steps echoed off the walls as if the place were empty, abandoned.

But his mother was somewhere. Still in her old rooms, probably. Aiden didn't want to think of her, of how helpless her condition rendered her. And him. It had been so long since he'd last heard her voice on the phone, right before her stroke two years ago. After the car accident made travel difficult for her, Aiden's mother had called him once a week—always when James left the house. The last time he'd seen Blackstone Manor's phone number on his caller ID, it had been his brother calling to tell him their mother had suffered a stroke, brought on by complications from her paralysis. Then silence ever since.

To Aiden's surprise, Nolen went directly to the stairway, oak banister gleaming even in the dim light as if it had just been polished. Most formal meetings in the house were held in his grandfather's study, where Aiden had assumed he'd be meeting with the lawyer. He'd just as soon get down to business.

"Did the lawyer give up on my arrival?" Aiden asked, curious about why he was being shown to his room first.

"I was told to bring you upstairs," Nolen replied, not even glancing back. Did he view the prodigal son with suspicion, an unknown entity who would change life as Nolen had lived it for over forty years?

Damn straight. He had every intention of using his grandfather's money to move his mother closer to her sons and provide her with the best care for her condition, much better than he could give her personally. He'd sell off everything, then hightail it back to his business in New York City. He had nothing more than a hard-won career waiting for him there, but at least it was something he'd built on his own. He wanted nothing to do with Blackstone Manor or the memories hidden within its walls.

Having followed blindly, he abruptly noticed Nolen's direction. Uneasiness stirred low in Aiden's gut. His and his brothers' old rooms took up the third floor. To his knowledge—dated though it was—only two sets of rooms occupied the second floor: his mother's and his grandfather's suites. Neither of which was he ready to visit. His mother's—after he'd had time to prepare himself. His grandfather's—never.

The lawyer, Canton, had said James died last night. Aiden had been focused on packing and getting here since then. He'd address what the future held after talking with Canton.

He directed his question to Nolen's back as they neared the double doors to his grandfather's suite, his tone emerging huskier than he would have liked. "Nolen, what's going on?"

But the other man didn't reply; he just took the last few steps to the doors, then twisted the knob and stepped back. "Mr. Canton is inside, Master Aiden."

The words were so familiar, yet somehow not. Aiden drew a deep breath, his jaw tightening at the repeated use of Nolen's childhood designation for him.

But it beat being called Master Blackstone. They shouldn't even have the hated last name, but his mother had given in to old James's demands. The Blackstone name had to survive, even if his grandfather could only throw girls. So he'd insisted his only daughter give the name to her own sons, shutting out any legacy his father might have wanted.

Aiden shook his head, then pushed through the doorway

with a brief nod. He stepped into the room, warm despite the spring chill of the storm raging outside. His eyes strayed to the huge four-poster bed draped in heavy purple velvet.

His whole body recoiled. Watching him from the bed was his grandfather. His dead grandfather.

The rest of the room disappeared, along with the storm pounding against the windows. He could only stare at the man he'd been told had "passed on." Yet there he was, sitting up in bed, sizing up the adult Aiden with eyes piercing despite his age.

His body was thinner, frailer than Aiden remembered, but no one would mistake his grandfather for dead. The forceful spirit within the body was too potent to miss. Aiden instinctively focused on his adversary—the best defense was a strong offense. That strategy had kept him alive when he was young and broke; it did the same now that he was older and wealthier than he'd ever imagined he'd be when he'd walked away from Blackstone Manor.

"I knew you were a tough old bird, James, but I didn't think even you could rise from the dead," Aiden said.

To his surprise, his grandfather cracked a weak smile. "You always were a chip off the old block."

Aiden suppressed his resentment at the cliché and added a new piece of knowledge to his arsenal. James might not be dead, but his voice wavered, scratchy as if forced from a closed throat. Coupled with the milky paleness of his grandfather's once-bronze skin, Aiden could only imagine something serious must have occurred. *Why wasn't he in the hospital?*

Not that Aiden would have rushed home to provide comfort, even if he'd known his grandfather was sick. When he'd vowed that he wouldn't set foot in Blackstone Manor until his grandfather was dead, he'd meant it.

Something the old man knew only too well.

Anger blurred Aiden's surroundings for a moment. He

stilled his body, then his brain, with slow, even breaths. His tunnel vision suddenly expanded to take in the woman who approached the bed with a glass of water. James frowned at her, obviously irritated at the interruption.

"You need this," she said, her voice soft, yet insistent.

Something about that sound threatened to temper Aiden's reaction. Wavy hair, the color of pecans toasted to perfection, settled in a luxuriant wave to the middle of her back. The thick waves framed classic, elegant features and movie-star creamy skin that added a beauty to the sickroom like a rose in a graveyard. Bright blue-colored scrubs outlined a slender body with curves in all the right places—not that he should be noticing at the moment.

Just as he tried to pull his gaze away, one perfectly arched brow lifted. She stared James down, her hand opening to reveal two white capsules. That's when it hit him.

"Invader?"

He didn't realize he'd spoken aloud until she stiffened.

James glanced between the two of them. "You remember Christina, I see."

Only too well. And from her ramrod-straight back he gathered she remembered his little nickname for her. That stubborn *I will get my way* look brought it all back. She used to look at him that very same way when they were teenagers, after he'd brushed her off like an annoying mosquito, dismissed her without a care for her feelings. Just a pesky little kid always hanging around, begging his family for attention. Until that last time. The time he'd taunted her for trying to horn in on a family that didn't want her. Her tears had imprinted on his conscience, permanently.

"Aiden," she acknowledged him with a cool nod. Then she turned her attention back to James. "Take these, please."

She might look elegant and serene, but Aiden could see the steel beneath the silk from across the room. Was there sexy under there, too? *Nope, not gonna think about it.* His strict, one-night stand policy meant no strings, and that woman had hearth and home written all over her. He wouldn't be here long enough to find out anything...about anybody.

With a low grumble, James took the pills from her hand and chased them down with the water. "Happy now?"

His attitude didn't faze her. "Yes, thank you." Her smile only hinted that she was patronizing him. Her presence as a nurse piqued Aiden's curiosity.

His gaze lingered on her retreat to the far window, the rain outside a gray backdrop to her scrubs, before returning to the bed that dominated the room. His voice deepened to a growl. "What do you want?"

One corner of his grandfather's mouth lifted slightly, then fell as if his strength had drained away in a rush. "Straight to the point. I've always liked that in you, boy." His words slurred. "You're right. Might as well get on with it."

He straightened a bit in the bed. "I had a heart attack. Serious, but I'm not dead yet. Still, this little episode—"

"Little!" Christina exclaimed.

James ignored her outburst. "—has warned me it's time to get my affairs in order. Secure the future of the Blackstone legacy."

He nodded toward the suit standing nearby. "John Canton—my lawyer."

Aiden gave the man's shifting stance a good once-over. *Ah, the man behind the phone call.* "He must pay you well if you're willing to lie about life and death."

"He merely indulged me under the circumstances," James answered for Canton, displaying his usual unrepentant attitude. *Whatever it takes to get the job done.* The words James had repeated so often in Aiden's presence replayed through his mind.

"You're needed at home, Aiden," his grandfather said.

"It's your responsibility to be here, to take care of the family when I die."

"Again?" Aiden couldn't help saying.

Once more his grandfather's lips lifted in a weak semblance of the smirk Aiden remembered too well. "Sooner than I like to think. Canton—"

Aiden frowned as his grandfather's head eased back against the pillows, as if he simply didn't have the energy to keep up his diabolical power-monger role anymore.

"As your grandfather told you, I'm his lawyer," Canton said as he reached out to shake Aiden's hand, his grip forceful, perhaps overcompensating for his thin frame. "I've been handling your grandfather's affairs for about five years now."

"You have my condolences," Aiden said.

Canton paused, blinking behind his glasses at Aiden's droll tone.

James lifted his head, irritation adding to the strain on his lined face. "There are things that need to be taken care of, Aiden. Soon."

His own anger rushed to replace numb curiosity. "You mean, you're going to arrange everything so it will continue just the way you want it."

This time James managed to jerk forward in a shadow of his favorite stance: that of looming over the unsuspecting victim. "I've run this family for over fifty years. I know what's best. Not some slacker who runs away at the first hint of responsibility. Your mother—"

He fell back with a gasp, shaking as his eyes closed.

"Christina," Canton said, his sharp tone echoing in the room.

Christina crossed to the bed and checked James's pulse on the underside of his fragile wrist. Aiden noticed the tremble of her fingers with their blunt-cut nails. *So she wasn't indifferent.* Did she actually care for the old buzzard?

Somehow he couldn't imagine it. Then she held James's head while he swallowed some more water. Her abundant hair swung forward to hide her features, but her movements were efficient and sure.

Despite wanting to remain unmoved, Aiden's heart sped up. "You should be in a hospital," he said.

"They couldn't make him stay once your grandfather refused further treatments. He said if he was going to die, he would die at Blackstone Manor," Canton said. "Christina was already in residence and could follow the doctor's orders...."

His grandfather breathed deeply, then rested back against the pillows, his mouth drawn, eyes closed.

"Can you?" Aiden asked her.

She glanced up, treating him to another glimpse of creamy, flawless skin and chocolate eyes flickering with worry.

"Of course," she said, her tone matter-of-fact. "Mr. Blackstone isn't going to die. But he will need significant recovery time. I'd prefer him to stay in the hospital for a bit longer, but..." Her shrug said *what can you do when a person's crazy?*

Something about her rubbed Aiden wrong. She didn't belong in this room or with these people. Her beauty and grace shouldn't be sullied by his grandfather's villainous legacy. But that calm, professional facade masked her feelings in this situation. Was she just here for the job? Or another reason? Once more, Aiden felt jealous of her, wishing he could master his own emotions so completely.

But he was out of practice in dealing with the old man.

This time, Christina retreated to the shadows beyond the abundant purple bed curtains. Close, but not hovering. Though keenly aware of her presence, Aiden could barely make out her form as she leaned against the wall with her arms wrapped around her waist. It unsettled him, distracted him. Right now, he needed all his focus on the battle he sensed was coming.

"Your grandfather is concerned for the mill—" Canton said.

"I don't give a damn what happens to that place. Tear it down. Burn it, for all I care."

His grandfather's jaw tightened, but he made no attempt to defend the business where he'd poured what little humanity he possessed, completely ignoring the needs of his family. The emotional needs, at least.

"And the town?" Canton asked. "You don't care what happens to the people working in Blackstone Mills? Generations of townspeople, your mother's friends, kids you went to school with, Marie's nieces and nephews?"

Aiden clamped his jaw tight. He didn't want to get involved, but as the lawyer spoke, faces flashed through his mind's eye. The mill had stood for centuries, starting out as a simple cotton gin. Last Aiden had heard, it was a leading manufacturer in cotton products, specializing in high-end linens. James might be a bastard, but his insistence on quality had kept the company viable in a shaky economy. Aiden jammed a rough hand through his damp hair, probably making the spiky top stand on end.

Without warning, he felt a familiar surge of rebellion. "I don't want to take over. I've never wanted to." He strode across the plush carpet to stare out the window into the storm-shadowed distance. Tension tightened the muscles along the back of his neck and skull. Familial responsibility wasn't his thing—anymore. He'd handed that job over to his brothers a long time ago.

Aiden realized he was shifting minutely from one foot to the other. Creeping in underneath the turbulence was a constant awareness of Christina's presence, like a sizzle under his skin, loosening his control over his other emotions inch by inch. She drew him, kept part of his attention even when he was talking to the others. How had she come to be here? How long had she been here? Had she ever found a place to belong? The heightened emotion increased the tension in his neck. A dull headache started to form.

"You knew something like this was coming, considering your age—" Aiden gestured back toward the bed "—you should have sold. Or turned the business over to someone else. One of my brothers."

"It isn't their duty," James insisted. "As firstborn, it's yours—and way past time you learned your place."

As if he could sense the rage starting to boil deep inside Aiden, Canton stepped in. "Mr. Blackstone wants the mill to remain a family institution that will continue to provide jobs and a center for the town. The only potential buyers we have want to tear it down and sell off the land."

Aiden latched on to the family institution part. "Ah, the lasting name of Blackstone. Planned a monument yet?"

A weary yet insistent voice drifted from the bed. "I will do what needs to be done. And so will you."

"How will you manage that? I walked out that door once. I'm more than happy to do it again."

"Really? Do you think that's the best thing for your mother?" James went on as if Aiden hadn't spoken. "I've worked my entire life to build on the hard work of my own father. I will not let my life's work disappear because you won't do your duty. You will return where you belong. I'll see to that."

Aiden used his hand to squeeze away the tightness in his neck. "Oh, no. I'm not buying into that song and dance. As far as I'm concerned, this family line *should* die out. If the Blackstone name disappears, all the better."

"I knew you'd feel that way," his grandfather said with a long-suffering sigh. "That's why I'm prepared to make it worth your while."

* * *

Christina listened to the men spar with one another as if from a distance. Shock cocooned her inside her own bubble of fear.

Aiden's gaze tracked the lawyer's movements as he spoke, but Christina's remained focused on Aiden. The impenetrable mask of rebellion and pride that shielded any softer emotions. The breadth of his shoulders. The ripple of muscles in his chest and forearms, reminding her of his strength, his dominance.

Could a man that strong prevail over someone with James's history of cunning maneuvers, both business and personal?

"Why don't you just lay it out for me," Aiden said, his voice curt, commanding the immense space of the master suite. A shiver worked its way down Christina's spine. "The condensed version."

This time, Canton didn't look to James for permission. Proving he learned quickly, he cleared his throat and continued.

"Your grandfather set up legal documents covering all the angles," he said, pulling a fat pack of papers from his briefcase. "It essentially hands you the rights to the mill and Blackstone Manor."

"I told you," Aiden said. "I don't want it. Sell it."

Christina's throat closed in sympathy and fear.

"We can," Canton said. "The interested buyer is a major competitor, who will shut it down and sell it piece by piece. Including the land Mill Row is built on. And every last one of the people living in those fifty houses will be turned out so their homes can be torn down."

James joined in with relish. "The money from the sale will make a splendid law library at the university. Not the legacy I'd planned," he said with a shrug. "But it'll do."

Canton paused, but James wasn't one for niceties. "Go on," he insisted.

Canton hesitated a moment more, which surprised Christina. She hadn't cared for the weaselly man from the moment she'd first laid eyes on him, and his kowtowing to James had only reinforced her first impressions. For him to resist the old man—even in a small way—was new. Maybe having to face the person whose life he was ruining awakened a small bit of conscience.

"If you choose not to take over, Mr. Blackstone will exercise his power of attorney over his daughter to place her in the county care facility. Immediately."

A cry lodged in Christina's throat before it escaped as she envisioned the chaos this would unleash, the disruption and danger to Lily, Aiden's mother. She'd cared for Lily for five years, from the moment Christina had received her nursing degree. But Lily had been a second mother to her long before that, the type of mother she'd never had. The last thing she'd allow to happen would be handing Lily over for substandard care.

Aiden's intense gaze swiveled to search the dark recess where she stood. The shadows comforted her, helped her separate from the confrontation playing out before her. But that intense gaze pulled her forcibly into the present. His brows drew together in concern, the only emotion to soften him so far. She could literally feel every time his gaze zeroed in on her—a mixture of nerves and a physical reaction she'd never experienced before today.

But then his eyes narrowed on his grandfather, his face hardening once more. "What would happen to Mother there?"

James smiled, as his hateful words emerged from taunting lips. "Christina, I believe you've been to the county care facility, haven't you? During your schooling, wasn't it? Tell Aiden about it."

Christina winced as she imagined what Aiden must be thinking. Only someone as manipulative and egocentric as James could determine that this scenario—disowning his own invalid daughter—was the best way to preserve his little kingdom. Her voice emerged rusty and strained. "It's gotten an inferior rating for as many years as I've been a nurse, and it's had regular complaints brought against it for neglect…but very little has been done because it's the only place here that will take in charity cases for the elderly or disabled."

"How do you know I don't have enough money to take away that option?" Aiden asked, a touch of his grandfather's arrogance bleeding onto that handsome face.

Canton replied. "You can try, but with power of attorney, your grandfather has the final say."

"We'll just go to court and get it transferred to one of my brothers."

But not himself, Christina noted.

"You can, and I can't stop you," James said. "But how long do you think that case will take? Months? A year? Will your mother have that long…in that environment?"

"You'd do that to her, your own daughter?" Aiden asked James.

Having watched him since she was a kid, instinctively knowing he was even more dangerous than her own family but drawn inexplicably by Lily's love and concern, Christina fully acknowledged what James was capable of, the lack of compassion he felt for others. He'd turn every one of them out without one iota of guilt, might even enjoy it if he was alive to see it happen.

She rubbed trembling, sweaty palms against her thighs. Would Lily survive the impersonal, substandard care at that facility? For how long? Although Lily was in a coma, Christina firmly believed she was at times aware of her surroundings. The last time they'd moved Lily to the private hospital for some necessary tests, she'd gotten agitated, heartbeat racing, then ended up catching a virus from hospital germs. How long could she be exposed to the lower standards at the county facility without being infected with something deadly?

As numbness gave way to fiery pain, Christina stumbled forward. "Of course he would."

She didn't mean for the bitterness or desperation to bleed into her voice. The fire that started to smolder in Aiden's almost-black eyes sent a shiver over her, though he never looked her way.

"You son of a bitch," he said, spearing James with a glare. "Your own daughter—no more than a pawn in your little game."

Christina's heart pounded as fear battled awareness in her blood. This man, and the fierceness of his anger, mesmerized her. She instinctively knew he could introduce a whole new element of danger to this volatile situation.

James punched the bed with a weak fist. "This isn't a game. My legacy, the mill, this town, must continue or all will be for nothing. Better two people pay the price than the whole town."

Aiden frowned, his body going still. "Two of us?"

Canton raised his hand, drawing attention his way. "There's an additional condition to this deal. You can accept all or nothing."

Dragging a hand through his hair once more, Aiden moved away, stopping by the window to stare out at the heavy rain. Lightning flashed, outlining his strong shoulders and stiff posture.

Canton cleared his throat. "You must marry and reside in Blackstone Manor for one year. Only then will your grandfather release you from the bargain, or release your inheritance to you, if he has passed on."

Aiden drew a deep, careful breath into his lungs, but one

look at his grandfather seemed to crack his control. Words burst from between those tightened lips. "No. Absolutely not. You can't do that."

James's body jerked, his labored breathing rasping his voice. "I can do whatever I want, boy. The fact that you haven't visited your own mother in ten years means no judge will have sympathy for you if you try to get custody." His labored breathing grew louder. "You'd do well to keep your temper under control. Remember the consequences the last time you crossed me."

Christina winced. She'd seen more than one instance of James's consequences—they hadn't been pretty. Lily had told her Aiden's continued rebellion had cost him access to his mother, and eventually cost Lily her health.

"Why me?" Aiden asked. "Why not one of the twins?"

James met the question with a cruel twist of his lips. "Because it's you I want. A chip off the old block should be just stubborn enough to lead a whole new generation where *I* want it to go."

The cold shock was wearing off now, penetrated by sharp streaks of fear. Nolen, Marie and Lily—the other residents of Blackstone Manor—weren't technically Christina's relatives. Not blood-related, at least. But they were the closest she'd come in her lifetime to being surrounded by people who cared about her. She wasn't about to see them scattered to the winds, destroyed by James's sick game of king of the world.

Besides, she owed this family, and the intense, dark-eyed man before her. Most of all, she owed Lily. Her debt was bigger than Lily had ever acknowledged or accepted Christina's apologies for. If being used as a pawn would both settle her debt and protect those she'd come to love, then she'd do it. Christina's family had taught her one lesson in her twenty-six years: how to make herself useful.

The lawyer stepped up to the plate. "Everything is set

up in the paperwork. You either marry and keep the mill viable, or Ms. Blackstone will be moved immediately."

A strained cackle had Aiden glancing at his grandfather. "Take it or leave it," James rasped.

Christina barely detected the subtle slump of defeat in Aiden's shoulders. "And just where am I supposed to find a paragon willing to sacrifice herself for the cause?"

"I'd think you'd be pretty good at hunting treasure by now," James said, referring to Aiden's career as an art dealer, already reveling in the victory they could all see coming.

"I've never been interested in a wife. And I doubt anyone would be willing to play your games, Grandfather."

Taking a deep breath, Christina willed away the nausea crawling up the back of her throat. She pushed away from the wall. "I will," she said.

Two

"Oh, and one last thing…"

When spoken by James, those were not the words Christina wanted to hear. She eyed the door to the suite with longing. Only a few more feet and she'd be free…

For now.

"A platonic relationship between you two isn't acceptable. My goal is a legacy. I can't get that with separate bedrooms."

Panic bubbled up beneath the surface of her skin until Aiden replied with a droll, "Grandfather, you can lead a horse to water, but you can't make it drink."

Even from her new viewpoint near the door, Christina could see the twist of James's lips. "My dear boy, lead a horse to water often enough, and it will damn sure get thirsty."

The bad part was, James was right. She'd only been in the room with Aiden for a half hour and the awareness of him as a man sizzled across her with every look. But sleep with him? A man who was practically a stranger to her? She couldn't do that.

But what about Lily?

Christina noted the fine tension in Aiden's shoulders beneath his damp dress shirt. The whole room seemed to hold its breath, waiting on someone to make the next move. But it wouldn't be her—right now, she had no clue what to do, what to think. She just needed out of here.

Echoing her thoughts, Aiden turned toward her and took a few steps, only pausing for a brief glance back at his grandfather. "I refuse to make this kind of choice within a matter of minutes. Or to let Christina do so. I'll be back later tonight."

Aiden's control as he ushered them both from the room intrigued her. What was really going on behind his mask of defiance?

Christina maintained her own poise until the door to the master suite clicked shut behind her. Then she stumbled across the hall to the landing as if she was drunk. Pausing with a tight grasp on the cool wood of the balustrade, she drew air into lungs that felt like they were burning.

She'd just volunteered to become Aiden Blackstone's wife. But considering James's final requirement, how would she ever go through with it?

Startled by the shuffle of feet behind her, she tightened her grip on the wooden banister. Knowing Aiden and Canton were approaching, Christina struggled to pull herself together. She needed to get through the rest of the afternoon without the veneer cracking.

Just as she turned back to face the others, Nolen appeared at the end of the hallway. The old butler's eyes carried more than their share of worry as he approached, but he didn't say anything. He probably knew every detail of what had transpired in James Blackstone's suite this afternoon. Somehow, he and Marie always knew.

From behind her, Canton's voice rang clear. "It's early still. We can go down to the probate judge's office now and get the paperwork started. You can be married within a week."

Nolen frowned back at the lawyer, his glower making her feel cared for, protected. It was a rare occurrence for her—she was used to being the protector—making it that much more appreciated. Her heart swelled, aching with love and worry of her own. She slowly shook her head as she turned to face the men. "I need to think. Some time to think." She struggled to clear her clouded thoughts. "And I need to check on Lily."

"She's fine with Nicole," Nolen said, extending his elbow so she could take his arm. Old-fashioned to the core. Her muscles relaxed; her smile appeared. He smiled back. "But we'll stop by if it will ease your mind."

Resigning herself to his help because she knew it would soothe his concern, she slipped her hand into the crook of his arm. They crossed the landing to the other suite of rooms on the second floor. With a deep breath, Christina paused to look back over her shoulder. "Aiden, will you come see Lily?"

He watched her from several feet away, hooded lids at half-mast, hiding the only thing that would showcase his emotions. "Later," he said, short and definitely not sweet. But his still features didn't tell her whether he simply couldn't face his mother or simply didn't care. He turned to Canton. "I'm not going anywhere until I've looked over those papers and talked to my own lawyer."

With a short nod, Canton moved to the stairs and started down. Aiden followed, his stiff back forcefully cutting off any approach.

Nolen harrumphed in disapproval, but Christina ignored him. Maybe she was imagining the loneliness in that brief look from Aiden, but he seemed cloaked in an aura of solitude. With a quiet knock, Nolen let them into Lily's suite, leaving the mystery of Aiden behind her.

Here, filtered sunlight illuminated lavender-flowered wallpaper and a slightly darker carpet, the soft decor far removed from the oppressive majesty of the opposite suite. The tranquility soothed Christina's shaky nerves. They passed through a sitting room with the television turned low to the sleeping area beyond.

Nicole, the housekeeper's grandniece, sat in the overstuffed chair by the adjustable bed James had specially ordered. She looked up from the thick nursing textbook in her lap.

"Come to check on her?" Nicole asked.

Christina nodded. "How's she doing?"

"Oh, the storm did neither of us any good, but after I did her exercises, she settled right down." Nicole flashed a toothy smile, bright against her tanned skin. "Her vitals are normal, so she's resting fine now. Still a little spooky, though, seeing her respond like that."

"Oh, you'd be surprised at the stories nurses have about comatose patients. It's a very interesting area of study." Christina should know; she'd studied every case history, textbook explanation and word-of-mouth example she'd been able to get her hands on. The stroke damage had healed; still, Lily had not come back to them.

"You're gonna make a wonderful nurse someday, Nicole," Nolen said, beaming as if she were his own grandchild.

"Yes, you are," Christina agreed. She'd encouraged Nicole from the moment the girl had come around asking questions about Christina's duties. Now the young woman was a nursing student at the university forty minutes away and helped Christina with Lily on certain nights and weekends.

Christina went through the motions of checking Lily's pulse while Nicole and Nolen quietly discussed some problems she'd had with her car this week.

Christina laid her hand on Lily's forehead, noting the normal temperature, and scanned the monitors beeping nearby through habit. But there, the professionalism ended. She leaned closer to Lily's ear.

"He's home, Lily." She sighed. "He doesn't like it, but for now, he's here. I'll bring him to see you soon."

There was no indication that Lily had heard, just the beeps of the monitors. Lily's thin, pale features never moved; her eyes never opened. But Christina had to believe she was happy to know her son was back under Blackstone Manor's roof. She wouldn't be happy about her father's machinations, though. To force two people to marry... Christina shivered as she remembered the feel of Aiden's intense gaze penetrating the thin veneer with which she protected her emotions.

The housekeeper's arrival drew her from her thoughts. "So what's this I hear about a wedding?" Marie asked, marching in, still dressed in the apron printed with the words "I make this kitchen hotter" the sixty-five-year-old wore whenever she knew James wouldn't catch her.

Christina wanted to groan. How had the news spread through the house so fast? Sometimes she thought the staff had the place bugged.

"It's more of a business agreement than a wedding," Christina said, a slight wave of dizziness rushing over her at the thought. *"If* there is a wedding..." She wasn't entirely sure Aiden would go through with it, once that hot streak of defiance cooled. Could she, if it gave her the legal right to protect Lily?

But she couldn't share a bed with him. Surely, they could get around that part....

"It's unnatural, is what it is," Nolen interjected. "Two strangers entering into something as sacred as marriage."

"And those words of wisdom brought to you by a lifelong bachelor." Marie grinned. "Besides, they aren't strangers. They've known each other since they were kids."

There were flutters of panic in Christina's chest as she remembered that last face-to-face meeting with a seventeen-year-old Aiden. She'd mooned over him from afar every time she came to visit Blackstone Manor. Sometimes the hope of seeing him had drawn her just as much as Lily's company, but that day had taught her well how little he felt for her. Whenever she'd come near him, he'd demonstrated the same unpleasant endurance as her parents, who also looked at her as a pest that they wished would disappear. He'd called her *invader* many times over the years she'd hung around, aching for a bit of Lily's attention. Yes, that was definitely how he'd seen her time here at Blackstone Manor. After that final rejection, she'd stayed as far away from Aiden Blackstone as possible.

Nolen wasn't letting this go. "It is unnatural, I'm tellin' you. This isn't a good thing. James is manipulating them, and Aiden, his own grandson, into marrying for his own damnable purposes."

"And what purposes would those be?" Marie asked, her hands going to her hips.

Christina's mouth was already open, but Nolen spoke first. "Building some god-awful legacy. As if he hasn't introduced enough unpleasantness into this world. He threatened his own daughter if they didn't do what he wanted."

"Oh, I bet that's all talk." Marie looked sideways at Christina with a worried frown pulling all her wrinkles in a southern direction. "Is this true? Is he forcing you into something you don't want?"

This was getting way out of hand—and way more personal than Christina wanted. "No. I volunteered. And nothing has been decided yet." *But I will take care of Lily—and all of you.*

Marie went on, her frown softening a little. "Maybe our Christina is exactly what Aiden needs right now. These things happen for a reason, I do believe."

Christina's heart melted with Marie's sugar-scented hug, but she doubted anything she did would soften the hardened heart of the Blackstone heir.

"You never know what might happen in a year," Marie

said with a sly smile. "Besides, family takes care of their own. She'll be fine here with us."

This conversation was almost unbelievable. If Christina hadn't been in James's room, she wouldn't have believed the situation herself.

Christina's mind echoed with Marie's words. A year was a short time in some ways, a long time in others. Would she come out on the other side whole? Or with a broken heart to go with her divorce decree?

As long as Lily and the rest of her family were safe and cared for, it would be worth it for Christina. Marie was right. These people were her family, as close as she'd come to having one since her parents had divorced when she was eight. Who was she kidding? Her family had never been real.

As a child, Christina's sole purpose in life had been as a pawn in her mother's strategy to extort more and more money from her father. That's where Christina had learned what two-faced meant—her mother all lovey-dovey when Dad showed up, abandoning her at her society friends' houses when she was no longer useful. A hard lesson, but Christina had learned it well.

She'd promised herself when she'd turned eighteen that she'd never go back to that kind of situation; never again have no value outside of what she could do for another.

So was she *truly* willing to become James Blackstone's pawn?

"When are you heading back? That Zabinski woman is killing me."

He didn't want to think about Ellen Zabinski right now. He had enough problems on his hands. After a solid twenty-four hours of thinking, Aiden knew what he had to do. He still didn't want to, but this choice was inevitable.

"I'm not."

The dead silence would have been amusing if Aiden wasn't in such a bind. His assistant Trisha's silence was as rare as some of the art he imported. While he waited for her to recover, he paced across his bedroom to gaze out the back window. He compared the view of the lush country yard, the gentle sway of the grass and tree branches in the breeze, with the constant motion of the city. The very sereneness made him want to fall asleep. Not in a good way. Why would he consider uprooting his busy life, even if it was only for a few months?

A myriad of reasons not to do this rambled through his mind—work, taking a stand against his grandfather's high-handedness, a lack of interest in the mill and a whole host of other things. Then his gaze fell on the chestnut-haired beauty strolling across the lawn to talk to the gardener. Christina smiled, stealing his breath. Her stride was sure, and those hips... As she spoke, her hands gestured with elegant grace to illustrate her words.

He should be worried about his mom—not her nurse. But as Christina looked up into the fifty-year-old weeping willow in the backyard, exposing the vulnerable skin of her throat, Aiden's mouth watered.

When Trisha finally spoke again, her words were slow and measured. "What's going on?"

"Let's just say, I will be stuck cleaning up family business for a while."

She wasn't buying that. "How long can it take to get the ball rolling on the estate? He had a will, right? Why would that require you to be on-site?"

"Yes, he had a will, but that's not really helpful since he isn't dead."

A single bout of silence from Trisha was a surprise. Twice in one conversation—a miracle. But she came back with her usual snarky humor.

"So are you trying to talk me into moving to the wilds of South Carolina? Marty wouldn't care much for that."

Just the thought of Italian-born-and-bred Antonio Martinelli in Black Hills was enough to brighten Aiden's day. "No, as amusing as that would be, I was thinking more along the lines of giving you an assistant and a raise."

Make that three spells of silence, although the pause was much shorter this time. "Don't tease me, Aiden."

"I'm not kidding," he said, feeling as if he should raise his hand in a scout-style salute. "You've worked hard, sharpened your own sales skills. I'm gonna need help to pull this off. We can do a lot by conference call and video chats, and I'll make a trip up there when necessary. But the majority of first contact and sales will fall on you."

Aiden ignored the surge of misery at the thought of being away from his business for long. But he wouldn't be out of contact. And he *would not* lose the gem it had cost him years of his life to build.

"It's only temporary," he assured his assistant and himself. "Just until I can get legal custody of Mother." But watching until Christina disappeared from sight, Aiden knew his motives weren't nearly that noble.

Turning away, he gave Trisha a brief rundown of his grandfather's demands.

"Whoa," she said. "And I thought Italian-American grandparents were demanding. That's crazy. Why would you go through with that?"

"At least a wife will give me a weapon against Ellen," he said, making light of his current struggle. Shivers erupted just thinking about the barracuda with whom he'd mildly enjoyed his customary night, only to have her decide once wasn't enough. She'd spent the last month making his life miserable. "How often has she called the office?" Aiden had blocked her from his cell phone.

"Oh, every afternoon like clockwork. She doesn't believe that you aren't here. I'm just waiting for her to show up in person and force me to pull out my pepper spray."

There was way too much glee in his assistant's voice. "Don't get arrested."

"I won't…if she behaves herself—"

Doubtful. But Trisha handled most situations with tact—even if she talked tough. "Do whatever you have to do. Maybe me being out of town for several months will help. In the meantime, you can forward *client* calls to my cell."

They talked a few more logistics, and Aiden promised to be in touch daily. Balancing two businesses in two different states would not be a walk in the park, but he was determined to hold on to whatever he could in New York.

His grandfather might take his freedom, but he would not destroy everything Aiden had worked so hard to build.

Three

Aiden's uncharacteristic urge to curse like a sailor was starting to irritate him. As he snatched one of the cookies Marie had left cooling on the kitchen counter, he contemplated the grim facts. His lawyer hadn't found a way around the legal knots James had tied. There wasn't evidence to have him declared mentally unstable. He was, but then he'd always been. If jackassery could be considered a mental condition. And any legal proceedings to steal guardianship of his mother would take too long. Aiden wasn't willing to chance his mother's health and well-being. He owed her too much.

So his bad mood was justified, but when he found himself stomping up the narrow back staircase from the kitchen, the taste of chocolate chip cookie lingering on his tongue, he knew it was time to get himself under control. After all, he wasn't a schoolboy or angst-ridden teen. He was a man capable of engineering million-dollar art deals. He could handle one obstinate grandfather and a soon-to-be bride—but only with a cool head.

As a distraction, his mind drifted to other days blessed with warm cookies, spent playing hide-and-seek or sword-wielding pirates on these dark stairs. The perfect atmosphere for little-boy secrets and make-believe. He and his brothers had also used them to disappear when their grandfather came looking for them. He'd often been on a terror about something or other. They'd sneak down and out the kitchen door for a quick escape.

Aiden stretched his mouth into a grim smile as he rounded a particularly tight bend. Escape was something he'd always excelled at. Except with Ellen Zabinski.

He didn't hear the footsteps until too late. He'd barely looked up before colliding with someone coming down the stairs. A soft someone who emitted a little squeal as she stumbled. Certain they'd fall, Aiden surged forward to keep from losing his balance. Christina tried to pull back, but her momentum worked against her. Hands flailed, finding purchase on his shoulders. Her front crushed to his. Their weight pressed dead against each other, stabilizing as two became one.

Everything froze for Aiden, as if his very cells locked down. He managed one strangled breath, filled with the fresh scent of her hair, before his body sprang to life. Her soft curves and sexy smell urged him to pull her closer, so much so that his fingers tightened against the rounded curves of her denim-covered hips. The soft flesh gave beneath his grip.

He'd been without a woman for far too long. That had to be why he was so off balance. His strict adherence to his "no attachments" rule had led to a lifetime of brief encounters. His last choice had been a wrong one, a woman who wasn't happy when he walked out the door the next morning. It had soured him on any woman since.

Darkness permeated the staircase, heightening the illusion of intimacy. His and Christina's accelerated breaths were the only sound between them. They were so close, he felt the slight tremor that raced over her echo throughout his entire body. It took more minutes than Aiden cared to admit for his mind to kick into gear.

"Dreamed up more ways to invade my territory, Christina?"

He felt her stiffen against his palms, tension replacing that delicious softness. Just as he'd intended.

Before he could regret anything, she retreated, stabilizing herself with a hand against the wall. "Aiden," she said, prim disapproval not hiding a hint of breathlessness, "I'm sorry for not seeing you."

I'm not.

"And for the record, I'm not invading anything. So I'd thank you to never call me by that stupid nickname."

It was a sign of his own childhood needs that he'd resented the attention she'd received here at Blackstone Manor when they were kids, enough to tease her with his *invader* tag. There had been times he'd felt as if she *had* invaded their chaotic life, garnering what little positive attention there was to go around. How he'd resented that. To the point that, one hot summer afternoon, he'd spoken harsh words he'd always regret.

"I'm trying to help, Aiden. I really am." Her voice came out low, intensifying the sense of intimacy.

He had to clear his own throat before he spoke again. "Why? I'm nothing to you."

"And I realize I'm nothing to you, but I care very much for Lily."

He could feel his suspicious nature, the one that served him so well in business negotiations, kick in. "So what's he have on you, sweetheart?"

Christina didn't pretend not to understand. "Lily."

"Why? There are other jobs, other people in need of a nurse."

Her glare was almost visible in the dim light. He should feel lucky he wasn't smoldering under that fire. Instead, a cool brush of air drifted over him as she shifted back on the steps. "If you had hung around over the past ten years, you'd know that Lily has been like a mother to me. Ever since we were kids." Pausing to swallow, she looked down for a moment. When she spoke, her voice was once more firm and devoid of emotion. "I understand what's being required of me."

Somehow that monotone didn't make him any happier than her anger, and he couldn't resist the urge to shake her out of it. "You'd sell yourself to a stranger for what, money? Hoping ol' Granddad will give you a piece of the pie if you work hard enough for it?"

"No," she insisted. "I'm *not* selling myself, but I will sacrifice myself to do what I think is right for Lily." She reached out in a pleading gesture, but jerked back as her fingertips brushed his chest. A deep breath seemed to stabilize her control. The professional was back. "It's my belief as a nurse, and as Lily's friend, that she's conscious of where she is. This house has been her sanctuary since her car accident. I can guarantee that removing her from here will negatively affect her physical and emotional condition. Especially if he puts her in—" a shudder worked its way over her "—that place. I'll do whatever's necessary to keep Lily out of there…. Will you?"

Aiden shifted his legs, wishing he could pace despite the confinement of his surroundings. "Would he really do that to her, you think?"

An unladylike snort sounded in the air, surprising him. But Christina obviously wasn't in the mood to pull her punches. "Have you forgotten that much already? He's only become more pigheaded through the years."

"You seem to handle him pretty well," he said, remembering how she'd stared James down over the medicine.

Her brow lifted in disbelief. "He only concedes to my medical expertise because he's afraid of dying."

"He's not afraid of anything."

"Actually, Aiden, deep down we're all afraid of something." Her shaky breath told him she was afraid of something, too, but she wasn't revealing any secrets. "Death is the only thing James can't outwit, outsmart or bully into getting his way."

Though he didn't understand why, Aiden felt a strange kinship tingle at the edge of his consciousness. She might look delicate, but Christina was racking up evidence of being one smart cookie. On top of that, a common bond tightened between them: Lily. He knew the source of his guilt—his obligation to his mother. Despite her words, he knew Christina's devotion to Lily wasn't just friendship; something else lurked beneath that fierce dedication. Was it just how good Lily had been to her? Or something more? He'd find out what was going on there. She could bet on it.

The sudden silence must have become too much for her, because Christina moved forward as if to continue down the stairs. The polite thing would have been to step aside, but the ache to feel that body against his once more kept him perversely still. She slowed within a hairbreadth, tension mounting once more. "Aiden?"

"So you're really willing to do this?" he asked, almost holding his breath as he awaited her answer. What delicious torture to spend the next year with this woman and keep his hands to himself. Could he? *This was a huge mistake.*

"I don't know. I don't think I can, you know, share a bed with you."

The way her voice trailed off told him how very uncomfortable she was, which only awakened images of making her very comfortable in a bed for two. But maybe he could find a way to make this work.

"Don't worry. I'll figure out a way around that."

"Do you have any other choices for a wife?" she asked. "I didn't really give you a chance to choose."

Arguments? He had a few, but none that were effective. Excuses? A whole hay wagon full, but none he dared utter in the face of the threat to his mother's well-being. Other women? He could think of many a delectable armful over the last ten years, but none interested in anything as mundane as marriage. He'd stayed far away from the home-and-hearth type.

"No," he conceded, then stepped aside to let her pass. "I don't think I could pay my assistant enough to move to the middle of nowhere and put up with me 24/7."

"It's hardly the middle of nowhere," she said with a light tone as she scooted past, brushing the far wall in an attempt not to touch him again.

Which was just as well.

She continued, "We might not have the culture of New York City, but there's still a movie theater, nice restaurants and the country-club set." She kept that delicate face turned resolutely away as he followed her into the soft afternoon light of the kitchen. "Not something I'm that interested in, but to each his own."

Interesting. "What do your parents think about that?"

"Who knows?" *And who cares,* her tone said. Could she really brush aside what her family thought that easily? Everything he'd seen since his return made him think she was family-focused. Her graceful appearance, fierce loyalty and career choice made her seem exactly like the marriage, kids and picket-fence type. All the more reason to keep his pants zipped around her.

What were they going to do about that bed? It was long moments later before she finally turned to face him, but for once the delicate lines of her face told him nothing.

"Honestly, Aiden, I want to help. This situation is uncomfortable at best, but for Lily…"

She'll do anything. Her earlier question rang once more in his ears: Would he put aside his own selfish wants, his own desire to run far, far away for the second time, for the needs of his mother and his childhood home?

Would he?

* * *

Christina picked her way down the damp concrete steps in front of the stately Black Hills courthouse. Thunderstorms had blown through during the night, leaving a cool breeze that rustled through the Bradford pear trees lining the square. Her trembling body felt just as jostled as she followed Aiden and Canton. Were her feet really numb or was that just the shock of signing the papers?

"It's official," the probate judge had said, beaming with the pride of initiating a Blackstone marriage.

Luckily, it wasn't truly official—she still had about a week before the marriage license came in to regain her senses, but picturing Lily at home, fragile yet safe in her bed, told Christina she wouldn't change her mind.

She couldn't turn her back on the friend who'd given up so much for her.

The three of them reached the bottom just as a group of local guys approached. Cleaned up from work in jeans and button-downs, they looked like what they were—small-town guys headin' down to start their weekend with some fun at Lola's, the local bar.

"Well, look at this, boys. It's Aiden Blackstone, back from New York City."

Christina cringed inside. Jason Briggs had to be the cockiest guy in Black Hills, and had the mouth to prove it. Not someone she wanted to deal with given her current edgy nerves.

"Jason." Aiden acknowledged the other man with the single, short word. From his tight tone, Christina guessed his memories of Jason were anything but fond.

"Whatya doin' back here?" Jason asked, as if it was any of his business. "Can't imagine you showing up after all this time for a pleasure visit." He glanced past Aiden to Christina. "Or is it?"

The guys with him snickered, causing Christina to tense. While Aiden didn't seem like the "let's solve this with our fists" type, Jason had been known to push lesser men over the edge. The differences between the two were clear. Aiden was perfectly at home in his dress pants and shoes, his own button-down tucked in and sporting the sheen of a silky material. He wasn't the old-school business-suit type, but he looked like a sophisticated professional, while the dark, stylishly spiked hair and his brooding look gave him that creative edge that probably had the women of New York swooning like Southern belles.

She knew she was.

But in the midst of the other men, it was like comparing dynamite to ordinary firecrackers. Jason and his crew might be the big fish in this tiny pond, but Christina put her money on the shark invading their midst.

The metaphor proved apt as Aiden ignored their ribbing with the confidence of someone who couldn't be beaten. "I'm here to take over my grandfather's affairs, now that he's become ill," he said with quiet confidence, not mentioning the true purpose of this little visit to the courthouse.

It was Canton who stirred the waters. "Including the running of the mill," he added.

Rumblings started from the back of the group, but Jason shrugged off the explanation with a smart, "Doubt he can fix what's wrong any more than a good ol' boy like Bateman can."

"Who's Bateman?" Aiden asked.

The men simply stared at him for a minute before Christina answered. "Bateman is the current day foreman at the mill."

"Check it out," Jason said, raising his voice just a bit. "Guy doesn't even know who the foreman is, and he thinks he's gonna stop all the bull that's been going on over there."

"I'm sure I'll manage," Aiden said, cool, calm and collected. Standing tall on the steps, his back braced and arms folded across his chest, giving him the presence of a leader.

Jason held his gaze for a moment, probably an attempt to stare Aiden down, then shifted his cocky eyes to Christina. A weaker target. She fought the urge to ease behind Aiden's strong back for protection. Jason was older than she was by a few years, but that hadn't stopped him from hitting on her when they were teenagers. He hadn't appreciated her rejection, and now enjoyed hassling her whenever they met. "I guess you filled him in, huh, sweet cheeks? Is that all you gave him? Information?"

Confident he'd gotten a few good jabs in, Jason decided he was done with them. With a self-assured jerk of his head, he got the whole crew moving like the lemmings they were.

Aiden watched them go before asking, "So he works out at the mill?"

Canton replied before Christina could. "Yes. His father is in management, I believe."

"That's not going to help him if he ever talks to Christina like that again."

Startled, Christina eyed Aiden's hard jaw and compressed lips. She'd never had a champion before, at least, not one capable of doing much in her defense. That Aiden would punish Jason on her behalf…she wasn't sure how to feel about that.

Christina frowned after the departing group. Maybe she had more of her mother's tastes than she'd wanted to admit. None of the local guys had ever interested her much. Jerks like Jason who thought they were God's gift to the women of this town didn't help. But Aiden's quietly sophisticated, confident aura made her stomach tighten every time she saw him. Which was trouble, big trouble. Especially when she started looking to him for more than just that tingling rush.

Glancing back at the men, she found Aiden watching her intently. Her cheeks burned. *Please don't let him be able to guess my thoughts.*

"What's he talking about?" Aiden asked.

Was he asking her? Why not the lawyer? But the direction of Aiden's stare was plain.

"Well, I know there've been some problems out at the mill. Strange things happening. Shipments delayed or missing altogether. Perfectly good equipment breaking unexpectedly. Things like that."

"Sabotage?" Aiden asked with narrowing eyes.

Canton broke in. "Absolutely not. Just a coincidence, is all."

But Christina wasn't about to lie to the person she hoped would be able to fix it. "Some people say it is. But there's no proof of anything. Still, people in the town are starting to get antsy, superstitious, worried about their jobs—"

Canton cleared his throat, shooting her a "shut your mouth" glare. "Everything will be fine once they realize a strong Blackstone is back at the helm."

Still, Aiden watched her, assessing as if he were cataloging her every feature. But then his gaze seemed to morph into something more, something she couldn't look away from as heat spread through her limbs like seeping honey. When was the last time a man, any man, had truly seen her? Gifted her with a moment of intense focus?

But Aiden's silvery-black gaze didn't hold desire—at least, not the kind that shivered through her veins. No, his eyes appraised her, calculating her value. Their shared look allowed her to see the moment the idea hit him.

Yes, she could be useful to a lot of people, but to Aiden in particular. She knew this town in ways he didn't anymore. And Jason had just proven that taking over the town's biggest source of income wasn't going to be easy. Small-town Southerners had long memories, and little tolerance for outsiders coming in to tell them what to do.

He didn't have an easy road ahead of him, but she had a feeling she'd just been chosen to pave his way.

Four

Christina enjoyed reading to Lily. Sometimes she would indulge in short verses from a book of poetry, magazine articles or a cozy mystery. Today the words from a story set in a small town like theirs eased over them both, until muffled bumps and bangs erupted from the adjoining room. She cocked her head, hearing more thumping sounds. A quick glance reassured her Lily was okay, so she set the book down and hurried through the dressing room.

The noise grew as she approached the door that led from Lily's dressing room to Christina's bedroom. What was going on?

Opening the door, she found herself facing a…wall? A mattress wall?

Going back through Lily's suite to the other exit into the hallway only gave her time to get good and angry. Nolen stood outside Christina's room, arms crossed over his chest. His closed stance matched his expression.

"What's going on?" she asked.

Nolen shook his head. "That boy. Master Aiden always was one to get something in his mind, and that's all she wrote…."

Alarm skittered through Christina. What was he up to? One step inside the disarray told her it was no good.

"Why are you rearranging the furniture in my room?" She didn't care that her voice was high-pitched and panicked. He could not do this. He could not simply move himself in without permission.

Furniture had been shoved aside, her bed taken apart and general chaos reigned. In the midst of it all, Aiden stood, legs braced. He wore almond-colored cargo pants and a blue button-down, sleeves rolled up to expose muscled forearms with a sprinkling of dark hair. A masculine statue in purple girly land.

He nodded to the delivery guys. "I think I've got it from here."

Christina practically vibrated as she waited for them to clear the room. Her eyes rounded and her throat tightened as the men took her old mattress with them.

"Thanks, Nolen," she heard Aiden say before the door clicked closed. Then he resumed his autocratic stance nearby.

"Don't you think we should have talked about this first?"

His insolent shrug matched his nonchalant attitude, which only upped her panic for some reason. "Why? You said you would go through with this for Mother."

She wanted to scream, but held on to her control for a moment more. "Yes, but not sharing a bed."

He was silent so long that she shifted uncomfortably. Finally, he said, "James will get his way—you said that yourself."

"But if we give him the marriage, maybe—"

"He doesn't want this half-done, Christina. You know that. But I'm not going to force you to do something you don't feel comfortable with."

She raised her brows, pointedly surveying her disheveled room. "It seems like that's exactly what you're doing. I'm definitely not comfortable with *this*."

"We each have a side. I'll keep my clothes and stuff upstairs, out of your way. This doesn't have to be any more intimate than two people sleeping beside each other."

She wanted to study his face, see if he really believed that, but she couldn't scratch up the nerve. Instead, she concentrated on maintaining what small modicum of grace she still possessed.

"Look," Aiden said, "if we're gonna do this, we've got to be all in. Either that, or get out now."

Christina glanced at the door to Lily's room. "No. I'm in," she conceded. But as she turned back to measure the queen-size mattress dominating her small room, she had to ask, "Couldn't you have bought two twins?"

His grin should be illegal. "Where's the fun in that?"

Christina shoved leaden limbs through the armholes of her nightgown and dragged it on. The day had been long, and an even longer, probably restless night lay ahead. Her emotional turmoil was compounded by worries over Lily, James's health, the bargain she'd agreed to and Aiden… always Aiden. Nicole had testing to keep her away for the next two days, but Christina looked forward to the nonstop vigil Lily's care required. Sometimes she wished taking care of Lily were a bit more labor intensive. It might help her think a whole lot less.

Her sigh echoed around her tiny bedroom. Soon she'd be the wife of Aiden Blackstone. The cocktail of fear, desire and worry bubbling through her veins might just be enough to keep her awake until then.

But hopefully not. She stared at the new queen-size bed that consumed more than its fair share of real estate. Great, another worry. How in the world could she share a bed with Aiden Blackstone?

Long moments spent unable to imagine such a thing convinced her to worry about it another day. Instead, she settled in and let lethargy weigh her into the mattress. *Please, just a few hours of oblivion.*

But before she could drift off, she heard a sound from

Lily's room. Christina's heavy head lifted. Again, that shuffling sound. Muffled by the dressing room that connected her to the suite, but there nonetheless. Had Nolen or Marie come to check on Lily before retiring?

A grimace twisted Christina's lips as she pulled herself out from the warm nest under her covers. In the two years since Lily's stroke, she'd often heard noises from her friend's room. Sometimes the others came to say goodnight. Sometimes a branch from the oak tree outside had scraped against the window. Sometimes she heard just the creaks and groans of a house that had seen a lot of living.

Each time, a small part of Christina's heart hoped it was her friend. That Lily had woken up and would walk in here to gift one of her gentle hugs and tell Christina she was okay. That she wasn't responsible for what had happened.

But it never came to be—and that broke Christina's heart.

A muffled voice sounded through the partially closed door of the dressing room, and Christina slowed, not wanting to interrupt. As she paused, the words "Hey, Mom," barely floated in and her feet rooted to the floor. Aiden? To her knowledge, he hadn't been to see his mother since he'd come to Blackstone Manor. But she'd hoped. Someday.

She knew she should leave, give him some privacy. Instead, she found herself easing up to the door and peeking through the opening into the room beyond.

Aiden hunched forward in a chair just on the far edge of the faint illumination from the night-light. Even in the deep shadows she recognized his long, solid build. His head hung low, and his shoulders slumped, as if a weight of emotion dragged him down. He remained silent for long moments, not moving, almost not breathing. It was hard to reconcile him with the virile man who had confronted her on the stairs days ago. Or who'd stood his ground against the derision of Jason and his crew.

Her thoughts cut off as he looked up, gifting her with the sight of his strong features and stubble-lined jaw. It intrigued her, that small sign of weariness, that little mark of imperfection on a man usually so perfectly groomed. Would it scratch her skin if he kissed her? His deep-set eyes barely glittered in the darkness, lending to the mystery, the hushed intimacy of the moment.

"I screwed up, Mom," he said, surprising Christina with not only his words but his matter-of-fact tone. "I left here a kid, full of anger and pride. I had no idea what that would cost me, cost us. But especially you."

He ran a hand through his hair, leaving it in spiky disarray instead of sculpted artistry. "You didn't blame me then, and you probably don't blame me now. That's the kind of person you are. But I blame me. Boy, do I—"

The small choking sound tore Christina's heart. She saw no evidence of tears, but the depth of Aiden's sorrow reached out from across the space separating them. She wanted to go to him, hold him and tell him his mother understood. Her foot moved before she realized what was happening and only by locking down her muscles could she stop herself.

Invader. Aiden wouldn't want her comfort. And if he knew the role she herself had played in Lily's accident, hers would be the last face he'd want to see right now.

"But I will make up for it. I promise you, you will stay in this house for the rest of your life."

I'll do my best, too, Christina thought.

He stood, hands fisted at his sides, but he made no move to approach the bed holding the ever-silent woman. "Grandfather thinks this is some kind of game, with him in the role of chess master. But it's not. It's an act of penance. After all, you'd just been to see me when you had the accident. Coming to me because I refused to buck the old man and come to you. Resisting him was more important to me than you were." Long moments elapsed when Christina could only hear the pounding of her heart.

His final words floated through the air. "I'm sorry, Mom."

He remained still for the length of one breath, then two, before he turned and walked away.

Christina didn't move. Couldn't leave, couldn't continue forward. She stood frozen, held by the realization that this might be a game to James, but Aiden was more than a willing player. His investment was deeper than she'd thought, and if he ever found out her involvement in Lily's accident, she would become the biggest loser of all.

Five

Almost a week after making his pledge to his mother, the marriage license arrived—and Aiden was royally screwed.

Oh, he would go through with it. In his gut, he knew this was the last thing he could do for his mother, one thing she could be proud of him for. She'd made her home here, been highly involved in the community, and she'd want him to care for it, too.

He couldn't promise her he'd stay. But he could get her safely settled and make sure the town remained secure. Still, his confrontation with Christina on the stairs taunted him. And the fire with which she'd argued with him in her bedroom—soon to be their bedroom—tempted him to enjoy everything she might have to offer. Which made it imperative to lay out some ground rules with his future bride, so they both knew what to expect—from this situation and each other.

Following Marie's directions, he found Christina in the back garden among his mother's irises, which were in full, royal purple bloom in the spring sunshine. She was sitting on a wood and wrought-iron bench, a truly genteel resting place in the shade of a small dogwood tree.

He marched up beside her and dug right in. "Look, Christina, in terms of this marriage, we should start with—"

"Good afternoon, Aiden," she said, squinting up at him in a way that wrinkled her delicate nose. "Won't you please join me?" She motioned to the matching bench opposite her own.

He frowned. "Christina, this is a business arrangement. We should treat it like one."

"Aiden," she said, her tone a mocking version of his own stern one, "we don't do business like that in the South. Or have you forgotten? Now stop being a jerk and sit down."

Her words brought on a mixture of irritation and amused admiration, but it was the haughty stare that cinched the deal, that had his blood pounding in all the inappropriate places. It was the same implacable look she'd given James, though this time, that arched brow almost dared Aiden to defy her.

So be it. He was a New Yorker now, but he hadn't forgotten how Southern hospitality worked. He forced himself to take the offered seat and studied his bride-to-be. "And how are you this afternoon, Miss Christina?" he asked with a cheeky grin.

His Southern-gentleman routine coaxed a laugh from those luscious lips, which emphasized the shadowy circles under her eyes. For the first time, he wondered just how much of a burden this marriage was on her. Did her family approve? He didn't remember much about them, except that his mother hadn't cared for either parent. They'd divorced when Christina was quite young, he thought.

Had they changed at all, like their daughter? He remembered her as a needy, clinging girl, always hanging around, begging for attention with soulful eyes that could rival a puppy dog's. Or maybe those memories were colored by his resentment that she actually got the attention, the positive attention he'd wanted.

Now there was nothing needy about her. The calm, capable woman before him was both admirable and frustrating. Still, he wanted to break through that mask and see the real woman underneath, the one he'd caught glimpses of when she'd defended his mother and insisted on doing what was right. That attitude was more than just the picture of Southern hospitality. She possessed Southern grit. He wanted to dig deeper, to learn whether her dedication to those around her could be transferred to a sorry SOB like him.

He shook his head. Nope, not gonna happen. When he finally walked away from here, he wanted it to be a clean cut. It was the way he lived his life: no attachments—not even to the woman he planned to marry.

That didn't mean he shouldn't learn more, if only to guide him through the next year. *Yeah, right.* But he pushed, softening his tone. "Are you ready?"

"I guess so," she said, though her gaze slipped away to the irises dancing in the slight breeze. "I doubt even real brides are ever really ready."

You're a real bride. Even as the reassurance leaped to his lips, he forced it back. "It'll be over soon. Before long, everything will be settled, I'll return to New York, and you'll be free again."

Those dark eyes, sporting depths that made him uncomfortably curious, swung his way. "What do you mean?" she asked, her brow creasing.

"Isn't it obvious?"

"Not from my side of the equation, it isn't." Her body angled toward his despite the carpet of green grass separating them. "How can it all be over? How can you take care of your mother and the mill from New York?" Those gorgeous brows lifted high. "And not break your end of the deal, because James isn't about to let you out of it."

Aiden put out a hand in a soothing gesture. "Calm down. I'll get Mother settled and a good manager in to take care of the mill. I know how to follow through—"

"But not how to follow the letter of the law?"

"James is playing dirty. I don't think I should be expected to stay spick-and-span."

"Your mother would expect it."

Her words shot an arrow of emotion through him that he couldn't name. But she was right. His mother had always expected them to take the right road, not the easy one. "Don't worry. By then I'll have found a way to break the agreement and clean up this mess."

For once, he caught just a glimpse of hurt on a face that was normally schooled with graceful care. "Thanks," she said with a dry tone.

"Would you please stop analyzing every word and just trust me?"

"I don't really know you. Why should I do that?"

"Because I know what I'm doing. Or I will—" Eventually, but until then… "My grandfather certainly thinks he can outwit the two of us. He's making us marry each other."

"Actually, he's only making you," she said, reminding him once more of the picture burning in his mind of her stepping from the shadows of his grandfather's bed. The echoes of her words still rang in his head.

"But are we going to let him continue to drive this boat?" Aiden asked. "I'd much rather be at the wheel."

She nodded, slow at first, but then stronger, as if she'd come to a decision. "Exactly what do you propose?"

"A partnership, a business partnership with a few key goals. No pressure for anything else." This arrangement would be more for his sanity than hers. As much as he knew he should not get on more intimate footing with this woman, he wasn't a saint. But he wouldn't be alone in that bed. And sex would only complicate his leaving all the more.

No woman should get married in scrubs, even if the wedding wasn't real.

There'd been no time to change when James had summoned her to the study earlier. She'd thought he wanted to talk about Lily or his health, but walked in to find a local judge with ties to James. Now she stood self-consciously, waiting for this drama to be over.

Aiden, on the other hand, looked much more put together in casual khakis and a slick black polo shirt. Even his hair was styled in perfect little spikes, while hers was pulled back in a thick ponytail because she'd been finishing up Lily's exercises. One could almost be forgiven for hating a man for being so beautiful.

As the judge's benevolent gaze fell on her, she felt a twinge of conscience. She knew it was nerves, but she wasn't quite sure what to do with it. Especially since there weren't any acceptable options she could think of to stop this wedding from happening.

Screaming as she ran from the room wouldn't be appropriate bride behavior. Lily had taught her to act like a lady. Maybe it was her mother's crazy genes trying to break through?

She avoided meeting anyone's eyes by cataloging the one room in Blackstone Manor she'd rarely been in. James's study. Tradition seeped from the woodwork, adding to the gloom. What did James so love about this oppressive place? Maybe that was it…the atmosphere only added to the power he wielded here.

Dark, mahogany shelves were loaded with perfectly placed leather-bound volumes. Heavy green drapes framed the three sets of windows in the room, the color of the material meant to reflect the landscaping outside. There was an impression of money and masculine strength, but not in a good way.

The lingering feel was one of suppressed power and manipulation, as if the meanness exhibited here had soaked into the wood, though maybe that stemmed from the similarities to her own father's office. He'd delivered many a harsh punishment from behind a desk similar to the ornate mahogany one dominating the far corner.

Suddenly, Aiden appeared in front of her, blocking everything from view but his silvery gaze. "Christina," he murmured, those mobile lips drawing her attention down, making her wish this was all real, even though she knew she shouldn't.

"You good?" The furrow between his brows deepened. "I mean, we don't have to do this right now if you don't want to."

Oh yes, they did. Before the nausea in the pit of her stomach got the best of her. The slight hope in his eyes made her sad. His face wavered for just a moment. "No, I'm fine," she murmured.

Nolen appeared over Aiden's shoulder. "Anyone you want to be here, Miss Christina? I could make a call."

She couldn't tell if the look of surprise crossing Aiden's face was because Nolen asked or because she might want someone here. The last thing she needed was one of her parents showing up. Her brother would consider this a waste of his precious time. Besides, the fewer people to know, the better.

At least for now. The truth would get out soon enough. It always did in a town the size of Black Hills.

She closed her eyes tight, letting the darkness shut out all the watching faces, then centered herself from the outside in. By the time her lashes lifted, she was back on track. "No, Nolen," she said. "All the family I need is already here."

Her eyes met Aiden's. "I'm ready."

As they settled into place, Judge Harriman studied her for a moment, as if he knew all the secrets she was trying so desperately to cover up. Not that everyone wouldn't eventually guess, once they knew she'd married the Blackstone brother no one had seen in ten years. Her pride was worth Lily's comfort.

"Let's get a move on," James fussed from his chair behind the desk. Christina could hear the shuffle of Nolen's and Canton's feet behind her.

For Lily...

"Dearly beloved, we are gathered here today to join these two people in holy matrimony..."

For Lily...

"Since it is your intention to marry, join your right hands and declare your consent. Do you, Aiden, take Christina to be your lawful wedded wife to have and hold from this day on, for better or for worse, for richer or for poorer, in sickness and in health, as long as you both shall live?"

Christina struggled not to wince. *For Lily...*

"I do."

Was it her imagination or did Aiden's voice echo through the room?

"Christina, do you take Aiden to be your lawful wedded husband..."

For Lily... "I do."

"With this ring, I thee wed...." Instead of looking at the plain gold bands that came from she knew not where, Christina started making a mental list of all the things she needed to do for Lily this afternoon. And tomorrow. And the day after that.

Finally, Judge Harriman put her out of her misery. "As you have pledged yourselves to each other before God and these witnesses, by the power vested in me by the state of South Carolina, I now pronounce you husband and wife. You may kiss your bride."

She hadn't allowed herself to think about this part. Luckily, Aiden had more sense than she did. His hand lifted to her chin as he turned to face her. Her mind registered the smallest details: how surprisingly rough his fingertips were, the difference in their heights as he leaned down, the first soft brush of his lips against hers....

For me.

Finally, her brain shut down, leaving only the feelings. The sharp tingle she hadn't expected, and the heat she had. But it was the urge to curl up against him that had her jerking away.

"Not as bad as you thought it would be, huh, boy?" James cackled.

The room righted itself, giving her a clear view of the disgust on Aiden's face as he stared James down—then licked over his lips. "Sweet," he said, though his expression was neutral. "Something you wouldn't understand, Grandfather."

All Christina felt then was the sting of the embarrassed flush creeping over her cheeks.

If the judge was surprised by the exchange, it didn't show. For once he ignored the old man. Pulling some paperwork out of his briefcase, he said with a grin, "Let's get this signed all official-like." Christina added her signature, which looked quite ladylike next to Aiden's masculine scrawl. Then the witnesses and the judge signed. They'd just tied everything up in a neat little legal bow when the door opened.

"Surprise," Marie said, wheeling in a tray with a three-tier—oh, dear—wedding cake!

Christina rushed over on the pretense of helping. "Marie, what are you thinking?" she asked, her overblown mind barely registering the chocolate and teal colors swirling over the layers like waves.

"What was I thinking? What were *you* thinking? Couldn't you have at least worn a nice blouse?" Marie tsked.

Christina tried to ignore the criticism, but found herself straightening the hem of her scrub shirt, anyway.

"Every wedding's a reason to celebrate, my dear," Marie said loudly, then continued under her breath. "Unless you'd like Judge Harriman telling people otherwise. There's a good reason Mr. James picked the judge with the most gossipy wife in town."

Christina nodded, but didn't answer. Her shredded nerves wouldn't allow it. She just cut cake and smiled, hoping she was making Lily proud. And safe.

No one pushed for the traditional "smoosh cake in each other's faces" move, thank goodness. Christina eased as far from Aiden Blackstone as she could get without raising eyebrows, but his warmth remained temptingly close. She wanted to lean in, share some of his strength, his outward calm.

Another kiss. But no. Not even while they were sharing that big ol' bed in her room. She would not get intimately involved with this man. It would mean nothing to him, and she knew herself well enough to know it would mean a whole lot to her.

How did people endure those long receptions after their weddings? It had only been twenty minutes of cake, and Christina was done. She gathered plates, helping Marie clean up while the men spoke in low voices. She was slicing cake for storage when she heard someone at the outer door of the house. Nolen had barely managed two steps toward the open doorway of James's study when a man filled it.

Luke Blackstone. Aiden's younger brother. He was known to be laid-back. He always had a big grin both in personal situations and when being interviewed on national television as a race-car driver. Cameras didn't faze him. He was always cool under pressure. And he'd become a sort of adopted older brother in the years Christina had been here. Among the three brothers, his visits home were the most frequent, allowing their childhood friendship to continue into adulthood.

"So." He grinned his trademark lady-killer smile. "What are we celebrating?"

He took in Christina, the cake, Marie and then the group of men at the far side of the room. His aqua eyes widened when he noticed his brother standing there. It took only moments for him to put two and two together. He was pretty, but he wasn't stupid.

Seconds later, he was storming over to his grandfather's desk. Hands planted on the mahogany monstrosity, Luke paid little attention to the papers sliding to the floor as he loomed over James. "What the hell did you do?" he growled.

Christina wanted to cry. Would the wedding-day horrors never end?

Six

"Now, explain to me one more time why we're at a bar on your wedding night?"

Luke might be a hotshot who had every woman in this bar sneaking a peek at what the tabloids described as his "dreamy" eyes, but all Aiden could think of at the moment was coldcocking him. Or shipping him back to Charlotte in his souped-up sports car. "Apparently, my wife thinks being here will keep her from having to face the new bed I moved into her room."

"Dude, if you're having to track down your wife, then this is gonna be one rough wedding night. Are you sure this marriage is real?"

"Oh, it's real." And more tempting than Aiden wanted to acknowledge. "And it's only temporary, but that doesn't change the requirements."

Luke's teasing turned serious. "I'm still trying to wrap my head around this. That's all. Make sure Christina is being taken care of, not just used."

"Thanks for worrying about *me*, your own brother," Aiden said.

"Oh, you're a big boy. You can take care of yourself, though obviously not very well."

The narrowing of Aiden's eyes should have warned him just how on edge his brother was, but Luke smirked it off. "Besides, if you wanted our help you would have called.

Jacob and I would have been on the first plane here. Why didn't you?"

"And have both my brothers witness my personal defeat? That would have been a fun family reunion."

"Still," Luke said, his gaze sobering even more. "We would have been here, you know that."

Aiden nodded. To add to his troubles, he could hear that asshat, Jason, running his mouth off at a table behind them. The young woman serving as bartender kept glancing in that direction with a worried frown, but Aiden had too much class to engage in a bar brawl with someone so, frankly, beneath him.

The difference in their stations had nothing to do with money, and everything to do with class. Jason had none. Aiden's parents had instilled the habits of proper public behavior from an early age. Aiden had refined himself even more as he moved among the highest circles of New York, and even international society. Besides, someone known to run his mouth in public was only going to damage his own reputation. Eventually no one paid people like that any attention.

As long as Jason kept it general and not too personal, Aiden would overlook it. He didn't want to start his tenure at the mill with the firing of a prominent, vocal citizen. But he had a feeling the time would eventually come when Jason would have to be dealt with—and Aiden would be more than happy to do it.

They thanked the bartender as she set Luke's beer and Aiden's Scotch before them, then sampled their drinks. "You hearin' much of that?" Luke asked with a jerk of his head in Jason's direction.

"Oh, there's plenty of insinuations and comments whenever I run into him and his little posse in town. He's careful not to be too direct. Everyone else just stares. No outright confrontations, but then again, Jason thinks he's big stuff because his daddy is on the management track out at the mill. I'm going to have to remind that guy of his place on the food chain. Soon."

"Let me know when that happens. I'm right there with ya." Aiden shared his brother's grin and fist bump. "But seriously," Luke said, "I haven't had any trouble the times I've come home and I haven't heard of Jacob having any, either."

"Yeah, but you didn't announce to them that you were taking over the main source of support for the entire town. I did. And I'm sure it spread like wildfire."

"So Granddad is really gonna let you do it? Take over the running of Blackstone Mill?"

"It's already done. I've been wading through paperwork for days and have a meeting set up with the day foreman next week."

A waitress rounded the curve in the bar with a full tray, pausing behind them. As she set their plates down, Luke asked, "Where's KC? I haven't seen her in a while."

The waitress's flirty smile faded into an oddly uncomfortable look. "Oh, she's been out of town for a bit."

Luke nodded and the men turned back to their food. As they dug in, Aiden's gaze was drawn again and again to a particular spot. He and Luke sat at one corner of a bar that formed a square in the middle of the room. Tables and booths filled the rest of the space, except for a small dance floor at the far end and a worn stage where a DJ mixed records. From where he sat, Aiden had occasional glimpses of some tables clustered together in the far corner near the dance floor, and who should be seated at one of them but his lovely bride.

Weren't they a pair? A real honeymoon should involve a bed and a shower for two, in Aiden's opinion. Instead, they were in the local bar. Separately. But then, this wasn't a true marriage, so he should leave all thoughts of a true honeymoon far, far behind him.

Still, as much as he wanted to deny it, saying those generic vows made possibilities available, intimate possibilities they shouldn't indulge. But the tantalizing options still lingered in his brain....

Being forbidden didn't stop him from watching, from imagining. She looked way too classy for this joint, even in a simple sundress that gave him a conservative glimpse of her creamy skin. But she seemed to fit, gifting that gorgeous smile to her girlfriends at the table and to the many who stopped by to chat. She was obviously well liked, just as he'd expected, and her generous nature made everyone feel welcome. Though he knew he shouldn't, he wished he could have a small amount of that genuine welcome spill onto him when he was in her presence. Instead, she guarded herself well, including running away on her wedding night. Not very far, but still—way to make a guy feel rejected.

"So what is the plan for the mill?" Luke asked. "If Jason is any indication, taking the reins might be a bumpy road. But I can guarantee in the end you'll be liked better than ol' James. Once they get to know you, of course."

Aiden grinned. "Would that really take much?"

"Nope."

Aiden didn't think so. "I haven't worked out the full strategy yet. Currently, I just need to solve whatever hoodoo is going on over there and install an overseer. Then I can hightail my ass back to New York City and get on with my real life."

"So you're going to win their trust, all the while planning to get out while the gettin's good?"

Well, when he put it that way... "No, I'm going to gain their trust so I know exactly what needs to be done to protect the town—from itself and any sharks that might want to come in. A strong management will keep everything on track, maintain the area's prosperity, and shut yahoos like Jason out. Then I'll know the right man for the job and everyone will get what they want." He tilted his Scotch glass in his bride's direction. "Christina will be helpful in getting people to accept me. Look how well she's liked."

"Yeah," Luke drawled, "people here love her. But for her to help, you'd have to persuade her to stay in the same room with you."

Aiden took a moment to indulge in a slap against the back of Luke's head—an older brother's privilege. Across the room, a waitress stood chatting with Christina, her empty tray tapping against her bare calf. "That table's been a revolving door tonight. All classes, too. That's hard to do in a small town."

"Especially *this* small town," Luke agreed. "But it's not gonna help you any if you're over here and she's over there."

Aiden glared.

Luke calmly licked some wing sauce off his fingers. "Just sayin', bro."

Was it time? Christina hadn't noticed him. He'd chosen this spot specially to watch her without detection. Give himself a feel for what she was really like, the side of herself she wouldn't show him. Now he couldn't stop looking that way, watching her sexy smile and the light glittering off her bare shoulders. How sappy was that?

After tonight, the whole town would know they were married. He was actually surprised it had taken this long. Despite his hard-nosed attitude about business, he wasn't a complete ass. He knew people needed to think their marriage meant something. At least while he was here. He stood, telling himself he was doing this because it was the best thing for his future. *Yeah, keep telling yourself that....*

"Go get 'em, tiger."

This time Aiden indulged in a harder slap on his brother's shoulder. "I will."

Leaving his brother rubbing the sting away, Aiden stalked across the room. He found himself ultra-aware of the eyes following his progress to the group of women in the far corner. Despite the music being louder here, he could almost hear the crowd suck in a breath and wait.

Finally, Christina's gaze stumbled on him…and stayed. *That's right, sweetheart. Found ya.* That baseline arousal, now becoming so familiar when he was in her presence, kicked in. His heart picked up speed. His muscles tensed. He could have been readying for a high-price negotiation or fast-paced auction, but the prize here could be so much more pleasurable if he let it.

Which he wouldn't.

He leaned in close, letting the end of a pop song cover his words. "Christina, would you care to dance?"

Panic widened her eyes and tightened her features for a moment before she shook her head. He didn't repeat himself. Glancing around the table at the women seated nearby and several more hovering, their avid interest unmistakable, he then let his gaze fall to, the bare ring finger of her left hand. "You sure about that?" he mouthed.

This time she placed her hand in his, allowing him to help her up. He led the way to the far side of the small dance floor, away from the now-whispering women. This side of the room was more sparsely populated, offering a small amount of privacy. The music had switched to a rare slow song, so he simply pulled her close and swayed. The point wasn't for them to dance, and the place didn't lend itself to fancy moves. He simply wanted them to be seen together, talking together, jump-starting the community's acceptance of them as a couple.

This had nothing to do with holding her. *Nothing.*

Unfortunately, Christina wasn't cooperating. Her back remained stiff, the muscles under his palm tight. He drew her a touch closer, trying to ignore the brush of her body against his. As if that was a possibility. He lifted their clasped hands to the crook of his shoulder. *God, she felt good.*

"You can loosen up, Christina," he murmured. "We are married, after all. And this is our first dance."

Which should give him the right to touch all the silky skin within reach. But it didn't. He needed to remember that.

Her fingertips dug into his palm. When she spoke, she was all politeness and concern. "I'm sorry. It's not you. I just haven't danced much."

He studied her, even as she refused to tilt her face up toward him. Instead, she stared into the distance over his shoulder. "So, why don't you tell me why you're spending our wedding night at a bar…without me?"

She shook her head. "It's not a real wedding night."

That bed says differently. "Is that what you want them to think?" he asked with a nod toward the bar.

"No." She stumbled a bit, brushing against him for a deliciously brief moment. "I just…I don't know."

Interesting. "Why did you come here tonight?" Of all nights…

He could feel her slight shrug.

Which wasn't really an answer, but he wouldn't press. He shouldn't want to know. He really shouldn't, but he could guess. After all, sharing a bed with an almost stranger couldn't be very comfortable. For her. It had been his M.O. for years, but the thought of Christina on that queen-size mattress felt nothing like the one-night stands that populated his history.

He found himself lifting her hands to his shoulders, guiding her where to place them. Then bringing her flush to his body. His arms encircled her easily, one hand resting just on the edge of the material of her sundress. Giving him his first true feel of the skin he'd been coveting.

Her eyes widened, but by degrees her body softened, inch by slow inch, as if she were sinking into him. It shouldn't feel so good,

"That's better," he said, his voice deepening, relaxing with her. "We don't want anyone to think you don't like me. After all, our news will hit the gossip mill any second now."

The luscious depths of her eyes were revealed by the gradual lift of her lashes, as if she was surfacing from a dream. "It would have already hit if Judge Harriman's wife wasn't out of town visiting her sister."

Aiden couldn't help but grin. "That's small-town life for you."

"Yeah," she said, sharing his amusement. "James didn't time his plan very well. But a woman has to see her sister every now and then."

As her grin matched his, he marveled at how natural it felt to hold her like this. To look down on her, shelter her against him. Warning signals were a muted clang in the back of his mind, overpowered by the blood thrumming through his veins. Of its own volition, his hand inched upward, sampling the bare skin along her spine, tunneling beneath that wealth of hair to find the sensitive spot at the nape of her neck. Her eyes lost focus as he stroked there. What would it be like to repeat this morning's searing kiss?

No. Not going there. James would be thrilled for them to get busy, make this a real marriage and provide him with another generation to control. But Aiden had no intention of sticking around long enough for that to happen. No matter how tempting his new wife might be. And no intention of letting his grandfather completely control his life ever again.

"Look, Christina," he murmured against her hair, "you don't have to be afraid of me. You don't have to do anything you don't want to. I know you didn't want the bed, but someone had to make the decision. I'm just trying to fulfill James's requirements and let you remain near Lily."

He felt her sigh against his throat. "So you were trying

to be gallant by moving a mattress in without my permission?" she asked.

He couldn't help teasing. "It's a comfortable mattress, isn't it?"

She pulled away enough to glare at him. "This isn't a joke, Aiden."

He paused, staring solemnly into those chocolate eyes. "I promise I will keep my hands to myself." Letting loose a little of the lust thrumming through his body, he added, "Unless you ask me not to."

Her lips parted, but no words came. Her expression was conflicted, and Aiden totally got that she couldn't decide whether to scold him...or take him up on the offer.

Lucky for them both, the song ended. The dance floor flooded with patrons ready to line dance, but "Boot Scootin' and Boogie" would not save either of them from the long night ahead.

Seven

Christina stared at the cabin she had completely forgotten existed. The last time she'd been this far from the house, shoulder-high weeds had curbed any exploration.

But the adult Aiden had been hard at work on the little cabin Lily had ordered built for him when he was a teenager. The immediate vicinity had been freshly cleared and lengths of unfinished two-by-fours had been used to replace the sagging porch. Old-school rock blared from inside. As she came around the corner, she saw a brand-new AC unit blocking the side window.

So this was what was holding Aiden's attention the past few days. Christina had been avoiding her husband, and memories of that embarrassing confrontation in the bar, for almost a week. Nights had been even more excruciating, but one or the other of them seemed to weasel out of being in the room at bedtime and wake-up time. Christina curled into a ball on her side to keep herself from brushing against Aiden in her sleep. Aiden, on the other hand, was more of a sprawler.

But she'd do anything to avoid a repeat of their wedding night. Aiden had entered the room just as she left the bathroom. He'd allowed his gaze to sweep over her sleep shorts and overlarge T-shirt with uncomfortable speculation. She'd scurried over to the bed and claimed her preferred side. But closing her eyes like a squeamish spinster had left her listening to the rustle of clothes as he undressed, her mind whirling with heated questions about just how much he'd left on.

Needless to say, she wasn't getting a lot of sleep. The days were only a little better. While Luke had been here, he'd served as a bit of a buffer, but she'd been glad when he went back to North Carolina because the speculative looks were killing her—she got enough of that when she dared go out in public. Considering the complicated web they were now living in, she couldn't blame Aiden for planning to spend a lot of time here. He probably needed one place that was solely his own. She wished she had one.

Noting the fence line indicating the end of Blackstone Manor's property and the beginning of mill land, she couldn't help but notice this was as far away from her as he could get. The realization lowered her confidence.

She knocked, then waited a moment or two. The music blared loudly enough to pound inside her head. After another knock, she forced herself to grasp the knob and turn.

Stomach churning, she stepped inside. Aiden stood in the far corner with his back to her. A back so smoothly muscled her mouth watered. His shirtless torso was magnificent. Sweat meandered down the indention of his spine and disappeared beneath the waistband of his loose khaki shorts. Muscles bunched and shifted in his arms and back as he wielded a chisel and hammer.

Before him rested a block of some kind of stone that he chipped away with focused intent. To her surprise, several other half-finished sculptures sat on other waist-high tables as if awaiting their turn. A cabinet in the middle of the room had various tools scattered across the top. Christina took it all in with a sense of wonder. She'd known Aiden powered a very successful import/export art business, but had no idea he created pieces himself. A twinge of sadness streaked through her that he hadn't shared this. But then, why should he? Just because she wished she knew him, didn't mean he felt the same.

Watching him move was like art in motion, the clench and release of his body mimicking the orchestrated roll of the ocean. Feeling awkward, she called, "Aiden." No response. Not even a twitch. She called his name again, raising her voice above the blare of Nirvana, but he still didn't turn.

She walked over and placed light fingertips on his bare shoulder. It was just meant to be an "I'm here" touch, but her fingers trailed down the slick skin of their own volition.

He glanced over his shoulder, his eyes faraway in a haze of glittering darkness. Several moments passed before he turned toward the stereo to shut it off. The slight frown between his brows confirmed her fears.

Her cheeks flushed, guilt creeping in as if she'd done something wrong. Not that she had, but words rushed out, anyway. "I called your name, but—" She gestured toward the player.

He set the tools on the table in front of him, then turned to give her a full tempting view. The chiseled muscles weren't confined to his back. His chest and arms suggested he was capable of some serious work without the bulk of heavy weight lifting, while his stomach gave washboard abs a new meaning.

She hadn't realized what those sophisticated clothes had been hiding.... She swallowed, drawing her eyes up before they strayed too far.

"No problem," he said, his voice even, reserved. "What can I do for you?"

She glanced around, distracting herself from all that skin by perusing the cluttered work surface.

"I, um, Marie needed to get a message to you, but she said there's no phone in here." She glanced back at his still features. "Didn't you bring your cell?"

He shook his head, reaching for a clean towel from a stack. "Too distracting."

He wiped the sweat from his face with a towel, then started on his arms. She swallowed hard, once again inspecting the tools and blocks of rock.

"I didn't know you sculpted. Lily never mentioned it."

He reached around her for the tools, putting them into a nearby box. "She's never seen my work. I didn't start until after her accident. It's great stress relief."

And Lord knew this was extremely stressful for them both.

She turned away from his intense stare, attempting to hide her trembling. She motioned to the horse he'd been working on. "I'm no art expert, but these look professional to me."

She felt, rather than heard, his approach. "It is. I sell my own work as well as other artists'."

He gestured at the blocks. "I had these brought over from the quarry so I could work until my assistant and I can arrange for a shipment."

Ah, a forceful reminder that he'd had a life before he came here. Unlike her. She should cut him some slack. Adjusting to a resented future was difficult. Even knowing that, she couldn't stop thinking he was standing awfully close....

"I'm glad you've got this..." She gestured forward. "I want you to feel at home—"

She clamped her mouth shut. That made him sound like a visitor. He wasn't. And she didn't want him to be. But after a lifetime of trying to appease and put people at ease, she simply had a hard time turning it off. And with him standing next to her, half-naked, she was only capable of reacting on autopilot.

"I'll never feel at home here." He shifted away, leaning

back against another workbench, putting himself unknowingly on display. "But I'm finding ways to make it work."

Did he mean his sculpting? Something of his own, uniquely his, to help him relax, relieve tension? Or something more? She should be thrilled that he was trying. Staying despite circumstances he hated.

Aiden broke into her thoughts. "What was the message?"

"What?"

"You said Marie had a message. From?"

Even those thick brows, simply raised in query, aroused her. "Bateman, the day foreman, called the house. He'd like to meet with you about things at the mill," she said.

"Did he really?" Aiden asked. "When?"

"This evening after shift."

His finger started tapping against his biceps. "So he wants to do this at the mill?"

She frowned at the odd note in his voice. "Yes."

The tapping accelerated. He was so different today. Normally, he walked around with emotions boiling beneath the surface like a volcano, but today he seemed to have mastered all that volatility. What was he keeping so locked down?

She found herself wanting to know more, to push deeper to places he'd say she didn't belong.

"The blocks," she said, grasping a subject from thin air. "How do you know what to sculpt? Client choice?"

She crossed to a half-formed block of black rock with goldish flecks. The top of a human head, thick with hair, had been roughed out, but for now all the fine details appeared below the chin. No features graced the face, granting no life to the form.

Reaching out, she traced the outline with her fingertips, noting how cool the rock was despite the heat in the room as the air conditioner slowly lost its battle. The texture was rough, but she could imagine the smoothness of such an elegant medium and form when it was complete.

Aiden had taken so long to answer, she thought for a moment he wouldn't. When he finally spoke, his voice seemed gruff.

"It's easy, really. You just have to listen."

She looked over her shoulder to find him watching her, or rather her hands. "Listen? To the stone?"

He trailed his gaze up her body before meeting her eyes. That turbulence of his seemed to be making a return. "Sort of. It's different for every artist. Most of the time I have a general idea of the goal. But the details change with the stone's intricacies and composition."

By now, she was sampling the textures with both palms. She could imagine Aiden chip, chip, chipping away, studying the angles until he found just the one that worked for him. The same way he approached life.

He wasn't the type to listen and work with an outside element. She smirked, her hands stilling. Of course, this was an element he had ultimate control over.

Suddenly, she was aware of that masculine heat at her back, blocking her in. Aiden's hands slid down her arms to cover her fingers where they curved around the rock.

His breath accelerated, stirring the hair lying heavy against the back of her neck. Tingles of fear and excitement made her heart race.

People might say he was a stranger, but he didn't feel like one. The aching need she felt around him had grown familiar. She'd spent long days thinking about him, long nights beside him feeding her fascination. Dangerous as it was, she didn't want to stop.

He leaned forward, trapping her between his hard length and the workbench. His arousal was unmistakable, subtly rubbing against her backside. She barely restrained herself from arching back against him. The need to respond grew despite her fears.

He pressed closer. With a groan, he nuzzled through the thickness of her hair, his movements slow, as if he acted against his own will.

The reluctant need echoed inside her, pulling down more of her barriers. She let her head tilt away, exposing vulnerable skin to his questing lips.

She shivered as moist heat slid along her neck, his open mouth sucking and nipping its way down. She lifted onto her toes. She was no longer thinking, just aching. For more feeling, more sensation, more Aiden.

His arms encircled her stomach, increasing her sense of security in the face of danger. Reaching the crook between her neck and shoulder, his teeth joined in play, his bite teasing, gentle. She jumped as the sensation shot straight to her core. Her body melted in surrender.

His hands slid upward, pausing just inches below her breasts.

Please, please don't stop. She wanted to cry out, but bit her lip, not quite ready to voice her desires. Her nipples tightened in anticipation. When he didn't move, she shifted, rubbing herself against him, an age-old move conveying her willingness for more.

Abruptly, his hands clamped onto her hips, holding her still. Her body and spirit froze in his grip as she realized it stemmed from something other than desire, despite the hardness still nestled against her.

All movement ceased except their breath. Christina fought the urge to move. As his mouth left her shoulder, she tracked his breath to her ear. Somehow, she knew she wouldn't like what he was about to say.

"Christina." Just her name in his rough tone sent shivers chasing across her skin. What would it be like if they were naked?

"Christina, you need to go." He shook his head against hers. "Now." More breathing. "Go. Now."

His hands tightened once more before freeing her, but she couldn't move. He might have told her to leave, but his body still cradled hers. He couldn't move away, either.

She should be humiliated at his rejection, but the evidence of his arousal bolstered what little feminine power she had buried deep down inside. Even knowing he would leave her far behind when given the chance, she wanted to risk getting burned, if it meant he would make her feel. She wanted him to let go and love her in a way she hadn't let a man do in, well, ever.

She turned her head and gathered every last ounce of courage to whisper, "What if I don't want to go?" Long moments lingered as her heart pounded in her ears.

Finally, he pulled away. "Then I have to be strong enough for the both of us."

Aiden drove to the outskirts of town in silence, Christina seated next to him in the cab of the estate's pickup truck. The awkwardness of their near miss in the studio earlier clouded the atmosphere between them.

But they both ignored it as he followed the newly installed signs pointing the way to the massive factory. Though mill property adjoined the grounds of Blackstone Manor, the roads leading there wound around and through the miles of land owned by the family. The drive took them along Mill Row, a sort of subdivision built on the border of mill land with houses for workers to rent, then through the fields behind Mill Row, which were used to grow cotton that provided a large portion of the mill's raw materials.

The closer they came to the actual plant, the slower Aiden drove. He'd dreaded this moment from his first step back inside Blackstone Manor. But he wouldn't allow himself to think about why. He certainly wouldn't explain his reluctance to the woman sending questioning glances his way. She had too much power over him already.

Besides, explaining his trepidation would require explaining why he'd asked her along. And what man wanted to be viewed as a wuss who couldn't face the site of his childhood traumas?

There were changes since he'd last been here. The parking lot had been widened and repaved. A new chain-link fence enclosure had been installed, along with a guard shack. But Aiden still viewed the metal buildings and now nonfunctioning smoke stacks with anger. To him, they would forever embody the oppression of his grandfather, even if they did keep the town viable.

They paused at the shack, but were waved through by a man Aiden didn't recognize. He didn't miss the surprise on the guard's face.

Once he had parked the truck, Christina got out and started forward but Aiden hung back. Each step was an effort of will. Either his body or his mind did not want to enter the massive building before him, but he refused to examine the source too closely.

Christina glanced back, her own steps slowing. "Aiden, are you okay?"

He didn't answer, but focused on moving one of his concrete-block feet one step at a time. He shouldn't stop, because he might not start walking again. But then his steps slowed to a standstill, anyway. His gaze strayed to the office building adjacent to the factory. His mind screamed at him to be quiet, but Christina's soothing, questioning presence pulled the answer from him.

"I haven't been here since the day my father died."

Her quiet voice reached him through the whirl of turbulence inside his brain. "I think you'll find a lot of people here remember your father. He did great things for the mill."

He would want you to do the same. Aiden gradually

picked up the pace, forcing himself to focus on his purpose. Not the images from the past crowding into his brain.

As they stepped through the entrance, they were met by a welcome committee of two. A man in a black jacket, looking more like a scientist than factory worker, stepped forward. "Mr. Blackstone, Mr. Bateman sent me to meet you. If you'll follow me, sir, I can drive you to his office."

Aiden waved him aside. "That's okay. We'll walk," he said, wanting to get an updated look at the operation. If this postponed his trip to the other building, that was no one's business but his.

The man blinked behind his round glasses as if he didn't know how to proceed now that his plans had been thwarted. At least he didn't seem inclined to argue.

The female half of the duo stepped calmly forward with her hand out. "Welcome, Mr. Blackstone. I'm Betty, Mr. Bateman's assistant. If you want to walk the mill floor, I'd suggest some earplugs."

Aiden accepted two pairs, handing one to Christina, who smiled at Betty in thanks. Then Aiden led the way out onto the mill floor, Christina, Betty and the little man trailing behind. The skin across Aiden's back tightened as he felt the eyes of their audience tracking their progress. He hadn't been out enough around here to realize he was living in a glass bowl. Christina's uneasiness reminded him that she was now living there with him.

But he forced himself not to hurry, strolling along the floor, occasionally asking questions of Betty. He spotted a production line undergoing some maintenance and spoke extensively with both employees about it. After exiting the factory floor, they wound through corridors for quite a ways. Aiden felt himself tense as they journeyed from the main action to the second story of the administrative building.

"This was built while my father was here," Aiden said, trying to moisten his dry mouth.

Betty answered, surprise in her tone. "Why, yes it was."

As soon as they crossed the heavy double doors into the administration building, Aiden felt his body's stress ratchet up a notch. His shoulders stiffened. He stared straight ahead, not looking down the little corridors they passed on each side. Finally, they reached the glass door marked Management. Betty led them through an outer office into a bigger room with casual office decor.

"Aiden, Christina, thank you for coming," Bateman said, shaking their hands.

Aiden watched as his wife was met with a warm hug, but his own greeting was more reserved.

"Betty had someone radio that you were walking the mill floor. What did you think?"

Aiden detected a note of pride, but also concern in Bateman's voice. "Everything looks good. The equipment has been updated."

Bateman nodded. "In the long run, it's more cost-effective to do so."

Aiden nodded, consciously tightening down on the grief hovering at the back of his mind. "How long have you been in charge?" He'd met a lot of men during his time here with his father, but Bateman's face wasn't familiar.

"Twelve years. I apprenticed under the man who took over from your father."

Aiden's shoulders tightened once more at the mention of his father, but he made a conscious effort to relax, stretching his neck to loosen up. "You've done a good job. The lines are running well."

Bateman indicated a sitting area. Hardly aware of what he was doing, Aiden guided Christina to the small love seat and tucked her close against him as they sat. Though he hated to admit it, the warmth where her thigh met his kept him focused. The tremors deep down inside receded, leaving him enough space to breathe. Contrary to his earlier actions, he needed her close, and for once his need had nothing to do with sex.

They chatted for a minute—Aiden well remembered Christina's lesson on polite behavior—then he got serious. "Before we start, there's something I'd like to address," he said. "As I'm sure you know, I've run my own business for several years now. An art import/export business out of New York."

He took close note of the defensive straightening of Bateman's back in the chair opposite them. Betty leaned casually against the edge of the desk in case she was needed.

"But a factory, especially a working mill, is outside of my experience," Aiden continued. "I've been studying my grandfather's reports, but I would appreciate it if you could fill me in on a few logistics of this type of operation."

Asking questions first rather than jumping in with orders appeared to be the right start. Bateman relaxed back into his chair, arms stretched along each side rest.

"The mill runs at full capacity eighty percent of the year, with some holiday and annual maintenance shutdowns. You may remember we carry out all production from the raw cotton bales to midgrade linens, so it is a large-scale operation."

He went on to explain about profits, which had declined the previous year due to drought, but were improving. Aiden listened attentively, but remained cued in to every subtle shift of the woman at his side. This split awareness was new to him. Normally, business always came before pleasure. But Christina could not be ignored. Pretty soon he wouldn't be sleeping at all. Her effect on him only grew. Good or bad, it simply was.

"Any financial concerns in the immediate or near future?" Aiden asked.

"No, sir. You'd have to ask accounting for specific numbers, but thanks to the long-term equipment upgrade schedule your father initiated and the profits reinvested, we've weathered through pretty well." Bateman's chest expanded a bit. "Our sales force has worked hard to establish a stable, loyal client base. We have no worries for the near future, outside of the normal business concerns in today's economy." A frown slid across his face. "No financial worries, anyway."

Aiden sensed they'd come to the purpose for this meeting. Christina must have, too. She leaned forward to join the conversation. "Is there something we need to know?"

Bateman's face was a guarded mask, as if he was deciding how much to say. He studied Aiden for long moments, until Christina spoke again. "It's okay, Jim. We wouldn't be here if Aiden wasn't going to do his best for the mill *and* the town."

Aiden wondered where her confidence came from, but didn't add his own reassurances. Bateman would have to take him on faith until he could prove his intentions himself.

When the older man spoke, each word came quicker than the last. "There is something off around here. Random problems cropping up. No pattern that I can tell."

"How long?" Aiden asked. The news wasn't unexpected, but he wanted details.

"Maybe a year," Bateman said, a frown of concentration on his face. "Little things, at first. But then the problems gained momentum, the worst happening most recently. A major supplier canceled at the last minute. One we'd been working with for a few years. Like everything else, it was an annoyance. But when they refused any further orders for no reason, it became a suspicious annoyance. It meant we had to delay a large delivery to an established client."

"If the mill gets a reputation for that sort of thing, it

could hurt sales," Aiden filled in what Bateman wasn't saying outright.

The other man exchanged a look with his assistant. "Did you show him?"

Betty nodded.

"We had a problem with one of the lines this past week," Bateman explained. "A delay because of equipment malfunction, but the tech came straight to me with his report. He thinks the failure wasn't an accident."

Aiden asked, "Any guesses as to who would do that?"

"Not the tech," Bateman said with a sad grin. "It could have been any employee with access to that area—part of the maintenance crew, or even the cleanup crew. I hate to think about it being any of those, really."

Aiden felt Christina straighten as the significance finally hit her. "You think it was an inside job."

Bateman nodded. "Unfortunately, yes. It was more an annoyance than anything, but I worry about the next time, if the source is who I think it is—"

"Why don't you just spell it out for me," Aiden said, absently laying a soothing hand against Christina's spine.

"About a year ago, a man named Balcher made an offer on Blackstone Mills. He's well-known in the industry for buying out the competition at rock-bottom prices and taking them apart, piece by piece, until eventually the plants just close."

"Eliminating the competition."

"Exactly. Only Blackstone isn't hurting. Yet. But if the safety standards are compromised on the equipment…" Bateman rubbed his balding head until what little hair was left stood on end. "I'm afraid someone will get hurt. Then we'll have more than our financial standing to worry about."

Aiden cursed. This must be the potential buyer Canton

had mentioned. The one who would destroy Black Hills, unless Aiden kept the mill viable. "Any suggestions?"

"Increase nighttime security?" Bateman said. "I'm worried about causing a panic, but I thought I'd tell the line managers so they could be more vigilant and strict about safety."

Aiden frowned. He didn't have much pull around here, but said, "I'll see what I can do about getting some authorities involved."

Bateman's face echoed his own worry. "I'm afraid it is time for that, though all I have is the tech's word. No real proof."

Aiden stood, shifting on the balls of his feet like a boxer. His mind worked over the puzzle. "If he's hiring inside personnel to sabotage the plant's effectiveness, you might not like what you find."

Still, he felt the surge of competitiveness rush through him. The grin he let slip out wasn't a nice one. "Too bad for Balcher, I'm not a pushover."

The tension in Bateman's shoulders and face eased, telling Aiden he'd gone up in the man's estimation. Good. They were going to have to work together on this. Teamwork? The loner Aiden balked at the idea, but this was bigger than just him and his own survival.

Though he knew he should be cursing a blue streak over this complication, instead, his energy surged. His competitive nature looked forward to taking Balcher on....

And winning.

Lost in his own thoughts, Aiden didn't realize Bateman was watching him with a speculative gleam in his eye. "Tell me," the other man said, "why are you doing this?"

"What do you mean?" Digging into motivation wasn't something Aiden enjoyed.

Bateman arched a gray-sprinkled brow. "You haven't set foot in this town since you were eighteen years old.

I'm smart enough to know you aren't here because you want to be."

"Then you are a smart man." Aiden dropped into a chair this time, letting his eyes drift shut against the glare of the fluorescent lights. He didn't want to focus too much on his surroundings and the memories they evoked. He didn't want to think about how alone Christina looked, seated there without him. He especially didn't want to think about how much he missed her warmth against him.

But Bateman wasn't finished. "You know, I was in upper management when your father took over direct supervision from James. I saw him in action on a daily basis. No matter why he came in the first place, your father stayed for one reason and one reason only. The people."

Aiden's eyes shot open, giving him a too-clear view of the white ceiling tiles. He wished he could throw out some quick, sarcastic remark, but his normally agile brain remained blank. "So what are you saying?" he asked, instead.

"That the two of you are a lot alike."

Aiden was ashamed to realize they weren't. He'd been so caught up in his own wants, desires and rebellion that he had hardly thought about others since that first afternoon at James's bedside. His father wouldn't be proud of the man he had become. Not at all.

As the realization threatened to close his lungs, Aiden knew he had to get out of there. Fast.

Eight

Christina had been so fascinated watching Aiden work, seeing his mind process the problems, that she wasn't prepared when he made excuses and motioned to the door. Her gears didn't change quickly, but the quivering urgency beneath his polite facade propelled her out the door ahead of him.

He turned the opposite direction from which they'd arrived, and his steps picked up speed.

"Aiden," she called. "Aiden, where are you going?"

She struggled to keep up, trailing behind by several feet. His steps were quick, and he never looked back. Her heart pounded. A seriously wrong vibe made the fine hairs on her arms stand on end. She followed him around twists and turns in the long hallways. Where was he going?

Finally, she rounded a corner to find him stock-still, arms and legs spread as if he'd jerked to a halt. His rigid stillness kept her silent, but she couldn't deny the impulse to get close. As she neared, she noticed fine tremors vibrating along his muscles. From the rigidity or something more?

Hesitant, she slowly extended her arm. This wasn't her place. He'd made it clear that she had no right to pry into his issues. Still, some inner need to heal, more intense than she'd ever known, urged her forward.

Just as her fingertip grazed his shoulder, he turned, blindly plowing back the way he'd come. And right into her.

He managed to keep her from falling on her tush. They danced a few steps until they collided with the wall. Their bodies came to a full halt, Christina's back braced, Aiden's arms on either side, facing her. His harsh breathing stirred her hair, awakening the urge to stroke her hands down his back until he calmed. Until he talked to her...

"Aiden," she said, aiming for a no-nonsense tone. He wouldn't appreciate emotion. "What is it?"

"I have to get out of here."

His voice was so strained, tight. She almost didn't hear him, he was clenching his teeth so hard. "Then let's go back through—"

"No."

She listened to his breathing a moment, searching for guidance. His straining lungs, tight fists and taut body told her he was seriously fighting for control over whatever was happening on the inside. Beneath the surface, something powerful was wreaking havoc.

"Why?" she whispered, her voice full of sympathy, coupled with something deeper, darker.

"I can't." He drew in a breath, flattening her chest against his. He kept his head facing away, shoulders crowded so close she couldn't turn to see. Finally, his voice came again, slow and reluctant. "I can't go back there. But I can't be here."

She wanted to understand, but felt as if she was navigating in the dark. So she did the only thing she knew how.

Reaching up, she placed her hands on each side of his waist, where his upraised arms left him vulnerable to her invasion. Her fingers traced the steeliness of his body under the thin cotton as she ran her hands over his ribs, then around to the bowstring muscles of his back.

Let me hold you.

For a moment, he ceased to move, to even breathe. Closing her eyes, she mentally sent out sympathy and peace as she'd learned to do long before her nurse's training. She could only hope to somehow restore his inner equilibrium through touch, physically and mentally.

He drew in a deep breath, easier this time, giving her hope that she might have reached him.

She inched closer, aligning her body with his, focusing solely on his breath as her hands slid around him. The intimacy of their position, of this situation, softened her voice to a caress. "Tell me what's wrong."

He held out, jaw tightened to trap the words inside. Her healing hands splayed across the small of his back. Her head tilted until her forehead rested on his chest, next to his pounding heart. Once again she sent the energy out, hoping for some kind of breakthrough.

"What's wrong?" he finally said, anger and bitterness giving the question bite. "I'll tell you what's wrong."

He twisted to point to the hallway he'd run from. "He died down there." She felt him shudder. "He simply stepped out of someone's office and fell to the floor."

She spoke despite her tight throat. "Your father?"

Aiden's nod shattered her control. She gazed into his taut face, darkened eyes, and felt the tears he refused to shed spill onto her own cheeks.

James certainly was a bastard. She'd thought he'd trapped them in a marriage they didn't want. She had no idea he'd sent Aiden back into his worst nightmare.

Aiden had little recollection of finally finding the exit door and getting to the truck. He wouldn't want to remember, even if he could. At least he hadn't blubbered like a baby. Running like one had been bad enough.

He'd just been sitting there, listening to Bateman talk about his father, and it had all become too much. He'd known if he didn't get out of there right then, things would get out of hand. Fast.

Before he'd come here, he'd gone days, sometimes weeks, without thinking about his dad. But now, everywhere he turned were memories of his parents, chipping away at the emotional control he'd built up all these years. Something he couldn't afford to lose.

Especially in front of Christina.

The familiar rhythm of tires on pavement, the mindless task of driving back to the manor, and the darkness helped him regain control. It didn't even slip when Christina spoke again.

"You were there...when he died?" He could hear the tears in her voice and wanted to tell her not to cry for him. But he didn't.

Surprisingly, he could answer without that gripping sensation returning to his chest. "He often took me to work with him that summer. I'd become too much of a handful for Lily at home, bucking James at every turn. She had her hands full with the twins, too. So he made me work down there as a runner for him."

He slowed down and pulled into the Blackstone estate, turning on the wipers as an evening drizzle started to fall.

"He'd just come out of a meeting when I met him in the hall. 'Hey, son.' That's the last thing he said before his heart attack."

Pulling around back, Aiden parked on the gravel lot outside the garage. The soft ping of water on the hood and windshield grew louder when he turned off the engine. Neither he nor Christina made any move to get out. The intimacy of dusk and the falling rain loosened his tongue.

"My father always had time for me, before we came here. He was a business-management professor for a small college. But James wanted Lily closer, and I guess my father felt he couldn't refuse the salary he was offered to manage the mill."

Put that degree to some real use, he remembered James

saying. But James had insisted on his old-fashioned ways and constantly found fault with the methods used by Aiden's father.

"Betty pointed out quite a few improvements your father made," Christina said. "Seems he was a good manager."

"I hope it was worth it," Aiden said, bitterness tightening his grip on the steering wheel. "The long hours and stress probably killed him."

They sat for long minutes in silence. Aiden's eyes drifted closed. The rain seeped down like the good memories, washing away those last dreadful moments: his father lifting him high in the air, explaining some kind of economic concept with apples and bananas, and grinning when one of the workmen praised Aiden. That's how he should remember his father.

It wasn't until his grip relaxed and his eyes opened that Christina spoke, "Ready to make a run for it?"

He grinned, his mood lifting as he caught the mischievous glitter of her barely visible irises. They'd had a bumpy road, but she had a way of soothing him. She seemed to know exactly what others needed in a given moment, and provided it if it was within her reach. It was so good, even while it scared the hell out of him.

He nodded, and they both opened their doors. Jogging out from under the trees, the rain fell harder. He hadn't realized how heavy it was until he was out in it. With his long legs, he could have easily outdistanced Christina, but he paced himself, only pulling forward enough to get the door open for her without breaking stride.

The kitchen was dark, the house quiet except for rain on the roof. They stood facing each other in the back mudroom, clothes dripping on the utility carpet, both looking like drowned rats. Christina's eyes met his. He couldn't resist a small grin at her soaked hair and the thin shirt now plastered over her very interesting curves. Her hands plucked at the clingy material, then she started laughing. Not the polite, amused titter of some of the society women he'd met.

Not for this woman. It was a deep, rolling belly laugh, doubling her over, making it hard to catch her breath. He couldn't help but join her, reveling in the lightness after the storm of his emotions. God, she was gorgeous. Even now.

"Marie is going to have a fit if we drip all over her kitchen floor—" she said.

"And the stairs."

She stuck her tongue out at his teasing tone. "You have farther to go than me, since your clothes are still on the third floor."

Even though *their* bed was on the second. And that's when it hit him. He was going to play, even though he knew he shouldn't—

"Not a problem," he boasted. Then he held her gaze for as long as possible before his shirt cleared his head. He dropped the material to the floor with a splat. Watching her closely, he noticed the smile had disappeared, and her gaze had moved down from his face. Even though his pants weren't nearly as wet, his hands went to the zipper. "You gonna join me?"

Her head was shaking before he even finished.

"You sure?"

Her gaze traced his pants' fall to the floor then traveled back up to devour the boxers he was left standing in. There wasn't any hiding his reaction to her interest.

"What's the matter, Christina? Scared?"

She stared at him, as if she was unsure how to take his question. Then she inched her bare feet—he'd missed her slipping off her shoes—toward the doorway. "No, I'm good."

Before he could stop her, she'd turned away. Her dripping clothes left a trail as she hightailed it for the stairs.

But she wasn't getting away that easy. His heart raced with anticipation as he followed. She was going to taste so good. So much better than the bitterness he'd forced down today.

His feet found the stairs, his legs propelling him after her. He heard her gasp right before he rounded the corner to meet her once more.

His voice growled from a throat tight with need. "These stairs hold the best surprises." Twisting her around, he pulled her off balance to meet him like the last time. His breath hissed through his teeth as her cold clothes pressed to his bare chest, but he didn't care. He was too busy anticipating her taste.

"Chilly?" she teased, but it didn't hide the way her body trembled beneath his hands. Then he was hit with her scent—jasmine or lavender, so soft he could breathe her in forever. Every centimeter of his body stood up and took notice.

He stared through the gloom. The wealth of hair—now curling in the humidity—hiding the vulnerability of her neck. The thin shirt outlining the soft rounds of her breasts. The pale skin of her collarbone. The awareness he'd been fighting since that first night exploded like a sizzle beneath his skin, loosening his control inch by inch.

Cupping her face between his hands, he whispered, "Not anymore," then drank from her mouth, letting the force of his desire push him beyond thinking.

Her lips parted. Her tongue met his, stroke for stroke, fueling the fire to an inferno. The feel of her delicate hands exploring his chest pulled a groan from him. "I need you, Christina. Now."

"Yes," she gasped.

Before he could lose himself in the feel of her body against his, he swept her into his arms. This was happening; nothing would stop it now.

His quick stride took them to the third floor and into his

room in precious seconds, leaving the chance of interruption far behind. Laying her on the dark navy comforter, he stripped her shirt off. The contrast between her pale blue bra and the dark background caught his attention; itches of possession tingled along his nerves.

With shaking hands he stripped her, uncovering the pale mounds of her breasts, which were more than a handful. Then he came to the silky slimness of her stomach, leading to rounded hips and the soft dark curls between her thighs. He moved to spread her long, toned legs, but she resisted.

"No," she whispered.

It took him only a moment to realize her fears. "Do you really need to hide from me, Christina?"

Her troubled gaze slowly zeroed in on him until he could see the moment she made her decision. This time he pressed firmly against her knees, not allowing her to hide. Exposing the softness between, he buried his lips against her. The greedy sounds of passion escaping from her throat ignited a heat under his skin. All thought ceased.

His whole being focused on bringing her pleasure. On the slick evidence of her passion. The silky lips of her sex. The tight arch of her back. The jerk of her hips as he concentrated in that most important spot.

All it took was one gasp, one short cry as she came to make him desperate to be inside her. Pulling back, he planted his knees in the mattress, forcing her even wider. As his body crowded over her, his mouth retraced his steps. He lapped at the delicate ring of her belly button, then along the line of ribs that heaved with her gasps for air. But it was her hands that pulled him higher. "Please, Aiden," she begged.

He made her wait a moment more while he drank deep and long from her lips, satisfying the thirst that had been building within him since the day he first saw her.

Her wicked hands explored his chest, nails scraping lightly over his skin until urgency rode him hard. "Now," she demanded, her voice strained with need. He wasted no time fitting his body to hers and pushing deep inside. Her soaked passage rippled around him, tight and unbearably hot. He could only savor her.

Don't think. Only feel.

For this moment in time, there was only the two of them working together. The lift of her hips driving him deeper with each stroke. The push of his thighs driving them both to a pleasure previously unknown.

He glanced down, and her wide-open stare caught him, the chocolate depths of her eyes holding untold secrets. As his body pounded into hers, that gaze wrapped chains around them that tied his soul to hers. He saw beauty, acceptance and the promise of rapture. She reached up to cup his face, fingers tangling in his hair as he burrowed deeper. Her eyes lost focus. Anticipation squeezed his lower back, his body pulling inward, readying for the leap. But it was the wonder in her eyes that sent him over.

With a groan, the tension exploded outward, leaving him shaken and useless. As if sex between them had drained every last ounce of rebellion and frustration, stripping away his starch. Limbs limp and sated, he sank over her and savored the long moments of quiet peace. Of relief.

A small jerk of her hips brought him back to the present. Reality flooded his mind in a rush: the quietness of the house around them, the darkness held off by the single lamp beside his bed, the unevenness of her breathing. The greedy gasp of the flesh surrounding his own.

Again his body hardened at the feel of the silken skin surrounding it, no barriers to dull the sensation—

No barrier!

With a mighty pull, Aiden separated from Christina and sprang from the bed. Her surprise slowed her reaction, granting him a glimpse of trembling breasts, pale skin marked by the rough touch of his fingers and the dark center where he'd found a peace unlike any he'd experienced before. Too soon, she jerked upright, reaching to push her thick, dark hair back from her face. He wished he could ignore her confused expression.

"What's the matter?" she asked.

Underneath the panic flooding his veins, his logical brain knew he was going about this all wrong. But when had he ever handled anything emotional right? He should be holding her, bringing her to another climax, not sinking into the depths of his own anger and fear.

"Condom," he said, passion still straining his voice. "I didn't use a condom."

Stalking to his closet, he yanked on underwear and then pants. "I can't believe I did that. What the hell was I thinking?" He jerked a shirt on in hard, short pulls. He'd spent his adult life avoiding commitment—especially a lifelong one like parenthood. As images of a pregnant Christina muddled up his brain, his voice gathered volume, "Tell me you are on the pill. Tell me."

His movements ceased abruptly when he glanced over his shoulder and spied the woman huddled in the middle of his bed. Her chin was tucked against her neck, her gaze pointedly fixed on the navy comforter she had wrapped around her naked body. The body he had just made love to, then left without so much as a thank-you-very-much. But he couldn't stop the freight train of his panic. "Tell me you are taking the pill," he insisted again.

He didn't catch her mumble. Striding across the carpet, he placed a firm hand under her chin, guiding it up until he could look once more into the gorgeous depths of those dark eyes.

She didn't even have to speak. He could tell by the way she shied away from his touch that she wasn't protected in any way. "Damn," he muttered, stumbling back on suddenly shaky legs.

"What is the matter with you?" she asked.

"This isn't what I planned. It isn't what I wanted," he said, more to himself than her. His brain shut down, as if it had been dealt one too many shocks over the last few weeks.

Hearing a rustle, he turned to find her standing beside the bed, gathering the length of the comforter around her curves. Her back was straight and tense, those tight shoulders reminding him of the time they'd first met as adults. The only contrast being the sight of smooth, pale skin that tempted him to throw his panic to the winds and reenter forbidden territory.

She walked to her pile of clothes and started gathering them up in her arms.

"Okay then, is this a bad time of the month to conceive?" he asked clinically, his nerves demanding some form of reassurance.

"It's a bad time of the month," she replied, though her voice sounded robotic as she tucked the damp clothes against her.

Allowing her a small modicum of dignity, he waited until she was almost to the door before pressing for more information. "Are you serious or are you just saying what I want to hear?"

She turned to face him, giving him a head-on look at the misery in her eyes. "Is being a jackass genetic for you?" Without another word, she turned away. He grabbed her bare arm, sucking in a breath at the chill on her skin.

"Christina, please. I know I started this, but I didn't mean to leave either of us with a child we don't want."

"How do you know I wouldn't want it?"

Shock held him immobile for a minute, then heat blazed across his body. And not the good kind. "Are you saying you *want* me to get you pregnant?"

"No, Aiden," she said, her voice steadier than before.

"I'm just saying I've always wanted children of my own. But you don't have to worry. I'll take care of everything."

He wouldn't have to worry? "I don't want children. Ever. When this is over, I'm heading straight back to New York. Not staying because I gave James another weapon to use against me. I have to get away." He would smother if he knew he was only here because his grandfather had tied his hands.

Her eyes closed for a moment, then that tight, haughty look slipped over her face once more. A mask that was achingly familiar.

She held herself away from him, preserving a few inches of space between their bodies. It only served to remind him of those moments just past when there'd been no space between them at all.

"I understand, Aiden. Believe me, I do. You'll get your wish. I promise."

Would he? Did it really matter in the aftermath of what they'd just experienced? Shame rolled over him as he watched her walk out of the room with quiet dignity, somehow graceful despite the improvised wrapping and his selfish commands. As his body demanded he follow and his mind demanded he stay away, he had to wonder what it was he really wanted.

Nine

Christina grasped the banister extra hard to keep herself steady. Walking with her head high down the main staircase, she forced one foot in front of the other. She refused to hide in Lily's suite, as much as she might want to. Hiding was for sissies. She would face Aiden like the strong woman she wanted to be, not the scared rabbit she'd been so often in the past.

Memories from the night before didn't make her walk to breakfast any easier.

From the moment his mouth had met hers, she'd been lost. All the heat, excitement and passion she'd craved her entire life had been contained in that kiss. It had been like coming home and finding all the holidays her family had neglected being celebrated all at once. Every nerve ending in her body had lit up, and thinking had become a thing of the past.

The part that had truly gotten under her skin had been the moment his gaze met hers. While his body drove deeper than deep between her thighs, his eyes had locked with hers for moments on end. She'd seen the man underneath, the same need for love and acceptance she had. The need to prove himself—not just to the world around him, but to himself. As she'd struggled to keep her eyes open, her gaze locked on his; she'd felt their souls touch in an intangible way she'd never experienced before.

Hell, birth control had been the last thing on her mind, even considering the complications of not using it. She'd known only the burn of Aiden's hard flesh inside her. Obviously, he'd come to his senses a lot quicker than she had.

And *she* was the one feeling awkward now. He hadn't come to bed last night, so she'd gotten a reprieve until morning. Still, she took a deep breath and walked through the door with even steps. Aiden was already seated at the table, sipping coffee and reading a newspaper. Business as usual. At least she wouldn't have to suffer as the sole focus of his attention.

Nolen hovered near the door to the kitchen and gave her a knowing look as he stepped forward to pour her coffee. *Dang it.* She'd love to know how they found out about things. Her cheeks heated. It didn't matter that she wasn't the one who'd stripped by the back door. She'd never have sex in this house again.

Aiden glanced over as she sat down. She ignored him, focusing on Nolen as he poured her coffee. "How about some waffles, Miss Christina?"

The thought had her stomach roiling, but even a nibble would be better than sitting there in strained silence. "That would be lovely, Nolen. Please tell Marie thank you for me."

With a nod, he left. Christina carefully poured cream then sugar into her cup. Today was for full leaded, not a halfway commitment. Waffles and sweet coffee. Screw her waistline.

"Christina, about last night—" Aiden began.

Of course he couldn't leave her in peace. Where was the fun in that? "Don't worry about it. It was a mistake. No problem."

"Of course it's a problem. I'm sorry—"

She wasn't sure if it was her angry glare or Nolen's reappearance that stopped him, only that she didn't have to hear more about what a problem she was. At least for the moment. Nolen lingered, to her appreciation, making sure she had everything she needed before reluctantly easing back over to the door. "I'll be nearby if you need me," he said, his tone strong, a little louder than it needed to be.

Her protector. She'd never had one before, but it sure felt nice.

Aiden studied her as she smothered the warm waffles with butter and heated strawberry preserves. The fruity aroma should have been tantalizing. Still, she forced herself to cut a bite and lift it to her mouth. Aiden spoke again as she chewed.

"Look, you're right," he said, much to her surprise. "I did say all the wrong things last night. I kind of freaked out—"

"Kinda?" she mumbled.

"But I want to make this right. We will be seeing each other a lot over the next several months—"

Not as much as she'd seen of him yesterday.

"—and I don't want things to be awkward between us."

Too late.

"So I propose—"

"You ungrateful, sorry excuse for a grandson!"

The interruption came from the hallway this time, leaving Christina disconcerted. At first, she had the horrible suspicion that James had found out about her sleeping with Aiden. Then she realized what he'd said. Why was he so upset?

Her stomach tightened. Confrontations had happened frequently when she was growing up and never ended well. James preferred his arguments loud and long.

Leaning heavily on a cane, he came through the door. "You think I'm already in the grave, boy?"

Aiden switched gears pretty quickly. "Hardly," he said, letting a wry amusement stretch the word. He'd turned toward James, but as she watched, he deliberately relaxed back into his chair.

"Oh, but you can ignore me, act like I don't exist, while you conduct my business right under my nose?" In his anger, James was unusually flushed and agitated. Christina's senses tingled as his left arm jerked a few times.

"Did you think I wouldn't hear about that little visit to the mill?" James winced, but he didn't take a step toward one of the empty chairs. "Don't you think you should have asked permission from the actual owner of the mill? Or are you trying to get in good with that day foreman while I'm too sick to stop you?"

"Why would you want to stop me? You told me to take over. That's what I'm doing, abiding by the *letter* of your law."

James grabbed Aiden's left arm, hard. Christina's sensibilities kicked into overdrive. "James—"

"By cutting me out of the loop?" James gripped his cane tightly, seeming to sway on his feet. "Taking meetings behind my back? I'm still in charge here."

As she stood, Christina felt an unnatural calm come over her. Gone was the frightened child witnessing one argument among many. The nurse took over, reminding her not to ignore her instincts. "James—" His color was pale but his cheeks burned red. He was definitely unsteady on his feet, but then he had been since his last attack.

Aiden found his feet, too, meeting his grandfather on equal ground. "You won't be in charge for long. Remember?"

When James's hand reached to press against his chest, Christina was around the table in seconds.

"Please, James. The doctor said you needed to stay calm. Let's just quiet down—"

"You!" James's focus finally shifted her way. "You're helping him take everything away from me. You should be grateful for all I've done for you. Instead, you're plotting to ruin me."

Christina wasn't sure where the paranoia was coming from. She didn't care. Right now, he needed calm and his medicine. But his next words halted her in her tracks.

"I should have known you weren't good enough for this job. Convenient, yes, but those scheming genes of your mother's had to show up sometime."

Christina swayed as all the blood drained from her head.

"Enough." Aiden's voice echoed off the painted paneling. "Bateman asked to meet with us at the mill. We went. If you want a report, I'll have it to you by this afternoon."

James looked like he wanted to say more, but winced, instead. Christina rushed forward, pushing everything aside but her training. "James. We'll get your doctor out here to look over you. Nolen!" she yelled.

James gasped, and panic spread across his face. "It'll be okay," she soothed. "Nolen, let's get him to the study and call an ambulance."

But James was having none of it. "No. Just take me back to my room. Dr. Markham can come."

"But, James—"

"No. No hospitals. If I'm gonna die, I'll do it at Blackstone Manor."

Two hours later, his wish came true.

Aiden stared at the monstrosity of a monument James Blackstone had erected for himself before turning away in disgust. He walked away from the crypt and the bronze coffin, leaving Christina behind as she greeted those still lingering at the graveside. Practically the whole town had attended the funeral, which made sense. The Blackstones were known by all. James would have expected the town to pay homage to him in his death.

Aiden just wished he could ignore the twinges of guilt James's death had given him. Those final words, spoken in anger, left him feeling lower than low. Which was just what James would have wanted. Aiden's emotions made no logical sense, but his grandfather had left him with more than one unwanted legacy.

As Aiden walked up the hill to the far corner of the cemetery, he shed the fake gratitude for fake sympathy that had soaked the last few days. Some of the ungodly tension he'd felt since he first walked back through the door of Blackstone Manor drained away. By the time he joined his brothers at his father's graveside, he felt marginally lighter.

James Blackstone was dead. For real, this time.

As much as he hated to celebrate a death, without James, Aiden would be free to do as he wanted, no interference allowed. Lily's guardianship would pass to him or one of his brothers, so James's instrument of punishment was removed. Aiden could legally start a trust and care for his mother, and find a stable management team for the mill. No one would be left hanging. Then he'd be free to return to New York and his business there.

If part of him cringed at the thought of never tasting Christina again, he refused to acknowledge it. Just like he wouldn't think about the last lonely nights back in his own room. In the long run, this was better for both of them.

"You hangin' in there, brother?" Luke asked as Aiden approached.

Aiden nodded, then turned to hug Luke's twin, Jacob. He had flown in as soon as Aiden contacted him about James's death. As the chief operating officer of a major manufacturing company in Philadelphia, he was as steady and by the books as his twin wasn't. The two men stood facing each other, looking like mirror images with their blond hair and suits. But Aiden knew the similarities ended there. Each twin was an individual, with his own strengths and talents, his own weaknesses. Today, dressed alike, with Luke's hair trimmed for the occasion, the differences didn't show. But they were there.

Blackstone Manor hadn't been home for him in a very long time. But anywhere his brothers were, he counted as his home. Despite living in separate cities, they came together for several days three to four times each year. Aiden and Jacob had dinner once a month or more, since they lived about two hours apart.

Aiden glimpsed his father's tombstone over his brothers' shoulders. How he wished he could talk to his dad one more time—get some guidance on where to go from here. His major instincts screamed at him to run, but he was more and more reluctant to do so. And that scared him.

He told himself he'd grown a soul. That leaving the people of Black Hills high and dry just wasn't what his mother would have wanted. But he feared his real motivations were much more complicated than that.

"Luke has been catching me up on all the drama," Jacob said. It wasn't surprising that the task had been left to his younger brother. Aiden had been running like a chicken with his head cut off since James's death. "Married, huh?"

Aiden nodded. "Not for long, I hope."

"I thought the deal was for a year. Besides, Christina is a lovely woman," Jacob said.

Luke snorted. "Damn straight."

"The deal was for a year while James was alive." Aiden mentally crossed his fingers, and refused to think about just how lovely Christina was—his brothers didn't need to know how far things had gone between him and his wife. "I'm hoping now that he's gone there's some way to untangle this whole situation. We'll meet with Canton tomorrow for the reading of the will, then I'll get my lawyer on it."

Jacob nodded slowly, his hand rubbing at the back of his neck like it did when he was thinking. He stared past Aiden at the gathering below them, but Aiden had a feeling he wasn't seeing much. Jacob was the problem solver of this little group. He'd been the one to find ways around

James's rules when they were kids, and viewed a multi-million-dollar problem as a simple brainteaser. So many times over the past month Aiden had picked up the phone to call him, ask him to get him out of this mess, but had always hung up.

This wasn't Jacob's problem; it was his.

"And what's the plan?" Jacob asked.

"I'm not sure about long-term care for Mom yet. The guardianship should transfer to one of us. I figured, when the time came, we could talk to Christina about options." And pray she didn't spit in his face when he walked away. As unsettling as the thought was, he was determined to go through with his plans. He didn't belong here. And he was quickly realizing that Christina deserved a lot better than the deal she'd gotten with him. "Without James here, I can visit Mom often, check in on her just like you all do."

He turned back to watch the remaining visitors clear the cemetery, leaving Christina standing with Nolen and the funeral director. A slight, warm breeze blew the silky black material of her dress against her legs, displaying an outline of full hips and thighs. "I'll need help finding someone to put in charge of the mill. With all the questionable stuff going on, we need someone smart enough to get ahead of the problems and hard enough to tell Balcher we'll never sell—and make him believe it. Someone who will work well with Bateman. Getting it done before someone gets hurt is my major priority at the moment." He'd worry about the personal issues later.

"I think I might have the man for you."

Aiden turned back to look at Jacob. "Already? Seriously, dude, you are scary sometimes."

"Not really. I want the job."

Aiden stared at his brother. Out of the corner of his eye, he saw Luke doing the same. "Why?"

"I've been thinking about moving back here for a while."

"And leave a successful career where you're making millions? Again I ask, why?"

Jacob shrugged. "It's personal, okay? I just want us to talk about it, see if that's an option."

"Is it? Of course. But I want you to be very sure." Aiden's arms crossed protectively over his chest, where hope was starting to form. If Jacob came home, Aiden could return to New York without any worries. Everything would be taken care of. Everything. *But what about Christina?* "I don't want anyone stuck where they don't want to be."

Luke pushed his way back into the conversation. "You mean like you?" he asked, eyes narrowed in a way that made Aiden uncomfortable.

Again came that twinge of uneasiness. Aiden ignored it. He'd made his intentions very clear to Christina from day one. "Damn straight."

Ten

Aiden pushed open the study door with anticipation sizzling through his veins. An older man stood at the far window. When Nolen had told him who was waiting, Aiden had been surprised. Leo Balcher's background and business had been an obsession since the trip to the mill. His showing up at Blackstone Manor and asking specifically to see Aiden was a stroke of luck. Whether good or bad remained unclear.

But it could give Aiden a chance to face off with the competition on home turf. He observed Balcher for a moment. The man's chubby hands curved around the carved wood borders of the shelves on each side as he surveyed the farmland as if he already owned it.

He was in for a rude awakening.

He turned as Aiden closed the door behind him, a too-jovial smile on his round face inviting Aiden to treat him like a good ol' boy. Unfortunately for him, Aiden hadn't bought into the old Southern traditions men had for interacting with each other before he left, and he wasn't about to schmooze and pat backs with Balcher. Having fought to earn his own way in a precarious profession, Aiden judged other men by the same standard of effort.

Comparing Christina and her sacrifice to some of the socialites he'd left behind in New York had him extending that thought to women, too. They might be on uneasy footing at the moment, but she was a woman worth more than many of the men he'd met. Including this one.

But Aiden wasn't above using Balcher's expectations against him.

Balcher crossed the room with his hand extended, his too-tight navy suit in stark contrast to Aiden's polo, khaki pants and hair still wet from the shower. Seeing Balcher eye his informal attire, Aiden barely suppressed a grin. Under normal circumstances, Aiden would never attend a business meeting dressed like this. But he was still more put together than the crew they'd met on the courthouse steps the other day. Wearing a lot less cologne, too. But Balcher probably counted on him being a pushover, someone who had no interest in professional behavior, when the truth was he'd been caught at an inconvenient time.

But Aiden wouldn't disabuse Balcher of his misconceptions. He'd use whatever advantage he could get.

"Mr. Blackstone. Nice to meet you."

"Please, call me Aiden," he said, enduring the man's hearty handshake. *Not really working, old man.*

"This is a beautiful place, Aiden," Balcher said, once again surveying his surroundings with possessiveness, only this time focusing on the dark, oppressive interior of the room Aiden had taken over as his office since moving back.

Taking in the heavy wood, curtains and ornate mirror, Aiden realized he really should gut this place and start over.

His lack of response unnerved Balcher, whose flashy smile was a little strained, giving Aiden a glimpse of too many teeth. He finally broke the silence on his own. "I hope the family is faring well, given the circumstances."

Aiden dropped into the creaky leather chair, leaning back to clasp his hands together over his stomach.

"Thank you," Aiden said with cool politeness…as close to chummy as he could manage. "We're doing our best. As you can imagine, there is a lot going on at the moment. Is there something I can do for you this morning?"

"I would have thought James mentioned me in some fashion, and my interest in Blackstone Mills."

He hadn't directly. Aiden had to find that out on his own. Bateman was right—Aiden's research showed Balcher loved to take the competition apart, piece by piece.

"I assumed this had to do with the mill, though I'm surprised you'd be here to talk business this soon after my grandfather's death."

The other man plopped his corpulent figure into one of the curved leather chairs facing the desk, adjusting his tie as if it was suddenly too tight. "No need to be so blunt, my man. Business should have its niceties. I simply prefer to get the ball rolling before other interested parties start moving in."

Aiden leaned forward, resting his forearms on the desk, and almost grinned as he echoed Christina's words. "Blunt is the way I deal—take it or leave it."

Regardless of his thwarted desire to settle the mill quickly and walk away, Aiden wouldn't have ever sold it to this man. Balcher wasn't being polite for manners. No, his attitude had a slickness and Boss Hog–style that spoke of greed, of consumption to the detriment of others. Besides, Aiden didn't believe in handing the lives and livelihood of people depending on him to someone he disliked on sight.

"Well, then, I'm sure your grandfather informed you of our discussions over the purchase of the mill and everything connected to it—"

"Marie told me we had a visitor, so I thought I'd bring along some refreshments," Christina said, easing sideways through the door. She carried an old-fashioned tea tray with a teapot, cups and some fancy-looking cakes. Aiden greeted her arrival with reluctant fascination.

He could look at her beauty all day, but he'd rarely seen

her since the funeral. Every room he entered she was just leaving. She'd taken most of her meals in Lily's suite, leaving him alone with his brothers. If she didn't relent once Jacob and Luke were gone, he'd be stuck eating alone.

And whose fault was that?

Having her here with her gracious movements and flattering smile was only going to distract him from besting Balcher. "That won't be necessary, Christina. Mr. Balcher won't be here long."

"Oh." She looked at them with dark eyes so guileless he immediately knew she was up to something. "Are you sure you won't have one of Marie's petit fours? They'll melt in your mouth, I swear."

The look in Balcher's eyes made Aiden wonder whether he was craving a cake, or Christina. Something dark and hungry rose in Aiden, taking him by surprise. He didn't need her here. She was a distraction from his true purpose, both professionally and personally. Was he hard enough to send her away?

"I don't believe we've met," the man said, clearing a spot on a side table so Christina could set down the laden tray. "I'm Leo Balcher, the owner of Crystal Cotton."

Hands finally empty, she extended one to their guest with all the graciousness of an antebellum hostess. "Hello, I'm Christina. Aiden's wife."

Eyes widening, the man looked from one to the other. "I was under the impression that all the Blackstone boys were single. Where'd he snag a pretty filly like you?"

Aiden's irritation kept growing, but he couldn't decide if it was directed at Balcher or at her. Or himself. He'd been on edge since the moment he'd left his bed with her in it. The days of deprivation since then hadn't helped.

What the hell was she up to? "Christina's a local," he said, watching her closely.

The man seemed to think the gracious Christina might

prove to be an ally. "Oh, well, I was just discussing the purchase of the mill."

She shot a quick glance in Aiden's direction, finally clueing him in. The woman who had dedicated her life to taking care of Lily and Marie and Nolen was concerned enough to take the weight of an entire town on her shoulders. He'd told her they'd work together, but instead of calling for her, he'd walked into this meeting alone.

Leaving *her* shut out.

Boy, he just kept being a bastard, didn't he?

"Balcher," Aiden broke in. "My grandfather is barely in the ground, and you are coming around to talk business? What was that about observing the niceties?" Aiden asked with a sardonic twist.

Out of the corner of his eye he saw Christina's shoulders relax, as if she realized he wasn't going to send her away anytime soon.

The man wiggled back into his chair, the joints creaking under his weight. "Well, now, you haven't been around these parts much," he said, his eyes shifting away from the intensity of Aiden's stare. "I heard there wasn't any love lost between you two. No reason for you to take over such a huge burden. After all, I doubt after living in New York City you'd be interested in settling down in the back of beyond." He smiled again, as if his rudeness made perfect sense.

"You're right. There wasn't any loyalty between my grandfather and I. Quite frankly, he was a sorry excuse for a dictator."

Balcher's facial muscles stiffened. Aiden hoped the other man was getting an idea of who he was dealing with now. Not an old man at the end of his life, but a young businessman at the top of his game. Though Aiden didn't want to tip his hand too quickly.

Maybe Christina would play the game, as well. She had trained her wide eyes on Balcher and was blinking as if confused. "What in the world would you want another mill for? You should have more than enough by now."

The little vixen! Digging for information on her own. He was perfectly capable of telling Balcher the deal would never happen and escorting him to the door. When the time was right.

She didn't trust him to do that.

Not that he blamed her. She had a huge stake in this venture. This town was her home; the people here meant a lot to her. She was justified in her interest. He just hoped she didn't steer the conversation away from where he wanted it to go.

"Well, my dear," Balcher was saying, matching her tone. Aiden began to feel like a drama was playing out before him, only the subtext was more interesting than the dialogue. "Competition is competition. It's a tough market, leading to tough decisions. Every mill can't stay in operation."

As Balcher's gaze inventoried the room once more, Christina eased farther into the background. Aiden's libido kicked into gear as he saw the emotions shift on her face. The same wave that had washed over her when she was defending his helpless mother. She was so passionate when it came to protecting others. Or when she was so pissed off that she forgot to be a polite little lady.

The temper churning in those chocolate eyes should not turn him on. Luckily, Balcher couldn't see it.

"But I understand Blackstone Mills is special." Balcher said, a small grin stretching his full lips. "And this house would fit me just perfect. I figured, after everything I heard about Aiden, we could come to some sort of compromise."

"I see," Aiden said, not giving the other man any clues. "What sort of compromise did you have in mind? After all, I think the manager, Bateman, is getting a little suspicious."

"Suspicious? What's there to be suspicious of? This is business, pure and simple."

Aiden saw Christina, now angled slightly behind Balcher, open her mouth to protest. He knew what she was thinking. That this wasn't business, it was people's homes and lives. *He* understood. But he needed to get information more than he needed to make a point Balcher wouldn't get.

He shot a warning glance in her direction before he said, "Well, you know that and I know that, but others don't. I can't stop Bateman from getting the authorities involved for long."

Balcher shifted his bulk from one side to the other. "Authorities?"

Maybe Aiden could push a little harder. "Well, you aren't exactly known for clean tactics, but equipment tampering could actually get someone hurt. If proof got into the papers, it could be seen as going too far. By some."

Aiden honestly thought Balcher's eyes would bug out of his pudgy, round face as he shot to his feet, but he slowly regained control. He thought hard for a moment before he said, "I don't know what you're talking about, but if this little problem gets to be too much for ya, I'll be happy to take it off your hands." He glanced out the window, absently rubbing his belly as if he was hungry. "It and all the perks that come with it."

"That's a shame, because it's not in the best interest of the mill or Black Hills for me to sell to a man like you." He grinned as he remembered something. "Oh, I'm sorry you've wasted your time." *There, niceties observed.*

Just as he made his way around the desk to escort Boss Hog to the door, it opened, and Nolen appeared. Was everyone listening in on this conversation?

"I'm just asking you to consider—" Balcher blustered as Aiden crowded him toward the exit.

Aiden must not have made his point clear. "I know what you want. We're not selling. Now get out."

Aiden didn't miss the satisfied expression on Christina's face. He only wished he'd had a more intimate role in putting it there. Too bad they shouldn't sleep together. Ever. Again.

But Balcher recovered fast. Reaching out, he offered Aiden a business card. "Well played, son. But you'll change your mind soon enough, when the problems only get bigger…and more expensive. Here's where you can reach me."

Aiden didn't hesitate. The card easily tore in half.

"I see," Balcher said. His eyes narrowed, his frown and frustration slipping through the good ol' boy facade. He turned slowly to look at Christina where she stood near the opposite window. Then he turned back to Aiden, the smile once more firmly planted on his face. "Just figured family would be the most important thing to you right now. Not some ol' business."

This time Aiden's inner alarms blared. Was that a personal threat? Was Balcher willing to get filthy dirty in order to get what he wanted? He glanced at Nolen, who had narrowed his gaze on their visitor.

Christina seemed to sense something, too, and all her sugary sweetness melted away. "Just what is that supposed to mean?" she demanded as she stalked closer, glaring with the same quiet stubbornness she'd used on James in his sickbed.

"Nothing, ma'am," Balcher said, all flashing teeth and concerned appearance. "I just know a brand-new husband like yours would be in full protection mode, that's all. I just figured he'd want to do what's best for y'all, town be damned."

Aiden wasn't buying the false concern. That hint of steel underneath Balcher's facade might make him harder to shake than he'd thought.

"I am," Aiden said, deciding he'd had enough formalities to last him an entire summer. "But I can protect my family *and* keep these people's jobs. Instead of turning the plant over to someone who will shut it down and sell it off as scrap metal."

Christina added, "Just like you did to the Athens Mill. Last year, wasn't it?"

Balcher didn't deny it, though he looked a bit startled.

The businessman ambled slowly to the open door, ignoring Nolen. Maybe he was tired of beating his head against a brick wall. Or maybe he'd decided to retreat and reassess his new opponents, opponents who seemed to have done their homework. But before disappearing, he glanced back at Aiden. "There may not have been any love between you and your grandfather, but you've got a lot of the old man in you, I think."

Anger and denial roared through Aiden for long moments after the door closed on that parting shot. When the haze finally cleared, Aiden swung back to face Christina. "What the hell was that? Waltzing in here with tea and cakes like this was social hour?"

Again that wide-eyed guilelessness, though Aiden detected a hint of uneasiness around the edges. "I don't know what you mean. I was simply being polite."

"You were spying. On me."

"Don't be ridiculous."

Some part of Aiden warned him he was taking his emotions out on an innocent, but he was tired of thinking when it came to Christina. He stalked closer, backing her up against the bookshelves. The soft smell of some kind of flowers wafted over him, but he ignored its soothing scent in favor of the anger driving him. Or was it something more, just as aggressive, but not as destructive?

"Let's get one thing straight, little girl," he said, resorting to the derogatory tone from that long-ago, childish conversation. "I won't be spied on, I won't be manipulated and I won't be played with. I got enough of that from my grandfather. I won't tolerate it from a wife."

For a moment, he could have sworn he saw a hint of that same emotion he'd seen so many years ago. Like a lost puppy being run away from a place she'd thought to call home. But whatever he'd seen disappeared in the flood of something far more potent.

Within seconds she was pushing back, practically standing on her tiptoes to get in his face. "Then don't be someone I have to spy on. Be open like you were at the mill. Work with me like you said you would."

Something primitive inside him sat up and took notice… of the dilation of her eyes when he leaned closer…of the uptick in the pulse at the base of her throat…of the tongue that sneaked out to wet her lips. *Careful.* It would be all too easy to slip back into her arms.

You did promise. Aiden wanted to ignore the thought, but he couldn't. Because he wasn't like his grandfather— no matter what Balcher thought. With a deep breath, he purposely moved their conversation in a safer direction. "I guess we do have a passable good cop/bad cop shtick goin' on."

Her eyebrow arched skyward, affording her a superior look that told him she still didn't trust him. She spoke in a low tone, but her words carried straight and true. "You could have sold it. Easily."

"To that guy? Unnecessarily cruel, I think." Aiden knew he should step back. Move away. But he couldn't.

She searched his face, probably hoping for reassurance, but as with Bateman, she'd have to learn to trust him from his actions. He just needed to give her something better to work with. Of course, if the reading of the will went according to his expectations, there wouldn't be a lot of time for her to learn. It was the reminder of the separation that was coming upon them so quickly that finally forced him to turn away.

As he walked back to the desk, she murmured, "The servants aren't the only ones good at figuring out what's going on around here."

"Don't you trust me?" Aiden could have smacked himself. He'd just decided trust was up to her, so why was he begging like a dog at the dinner table?

He barely heard her reply. "Should I?"

With those two words she conjured up memories of things he should definitely forget. Warm skin. Eager hands. Willing flesh. Everything he needed to stay far away from.

She glanced at her watch. "Look, I need to check in on Lily."

Something deep inside him protested. This might be his last chance to have her to himself. After their meeting with Canton… "What about you? Are you okay?"

She turned her head toward him by slow increments. "Are you worried about me? Or whether I'll make things more of a hassle for you?"

"These past few days have been crazy," he deflected. "They're about to get crazier."

"Why?"

"Now that James is dead, we can get this all sorted out," he said, gesturing between them. "Behind us."

He could tell the moment she realized what he was talking about. Not because of the emotion on her face, but because all expression disappeared. She nodded. "You'll be glad to get back to New York."

"It's where I belong."

She studied him for the course of several breaths. "Are you sure about that?"

Eleven

Christina stalled as she entered the study. She was the last to arrive, thanks to lingering with Lily and Nicole for longer than she planned. Avoiding the inevitable, as if that was possible. After all, will or not, Aiden would leave. His smooth good looks and smoldering intensity had seduced her into forgetting that. Too bad his temperamental attitudes weren't enough to cool her newly awakened libido.

She paused beside Nolen, whom she'd been worried about since James's death. "How are you holding up, Nolen?"

The butler rested sad eyes on her. "I know it was his time, Miss Christina. But this will be a big change."

"Yes." A delicate shudder shook her body. "Yes, it will."

Aiden moved closer, pausing nearby as if he wanted a word with her, but she studiously ignored him. The meeting with Balcher had been an emotional roller coaster, with another one directly in front of her. Coping with Aiden one-on-one wasn't a good idea right now.

As Canton gathered the papers out of his briefcase, Christina made her way to the couch and chose a seat next to Luke, who smiled in welcome. Let Aiden think what he would. It was way past time for her to stop caring.

Only family was there—or what Christina would consider family. Each grandson, herself, Nolen and Marie. No outsiders. Her stomach tightened. Did that mean the will was James's way of controlling them still? Had he refrained from airing their dirty laundry to others? Suddenly, her fears for the future were magnified.

She'd never trusted him—never in life, and not in death. It was a chronic issue with her and the Blackstone males, it seemed. But with Lily as a factor, there was no way to turn her back on whatever was coming their way.

Lily was all that mattered now. Not Christina's breaking heart, nor Aiden's damnable pride. Only Lily—the woman who'd sacrificed everything for those she loved.

Chatter continued at a low volume until Canton tapped his stack of papers against the desk. "As you can imagine from your dealings with him in life," Canton began, "James left extensive instructions about how things will continue after his demise."

Christina's sense of unease escalated, growing even worse as those around her shifted in their chairs. Whatever was coming, Canton knew. The knowledge shone in those beady little eyes behind his glasses. Christina got the impression he was about to have a taste of the power he'd been hungering for while James was alive.

She sure hoped that power was short-lived.

"Would you like me to read the will verbatim or give you an overview?" The little weasel's chin tipped up.

"Just tell us how we can unravel this tangle James created…my mother, the mill, this marriage," Aiden demanded.

Christina tried not to care about being classified as part of a *tangle,* especially since she could understand why Aiden felt that way. Besides, people had viewed her as a complication her entire life. So she pretended it didn't hurt worse than all the other times before.

"Divorce proceedings are easy enough to initiate," Jacob said.

Christina sensed Aiden shift forward in his chair. "Yeah, but that could leave Christina in an awkward position when all is said and done," he said,

She breathed deep. This discussion had to happen, even if it hurt her. She'd rather it be in public than privately between just her and Aiden.

Luke chimed in. "What about one of those annulment things?"

"Would be even easier," Jacob agreed.

"Yes," Canton said. "An annulment would be easy enough, provided you qualify."

He turned his gaze to her, staring as if he could tunnel beneath her cracking facade. In that moment, it felt as if every eye in the room shifted her way and heat flashed over her face. She wasn't sure where her protest came from, but she wished she could take the little sound back with all her heart.

Canton raised a superior brow, satisfaction in his small smile. "But I'm assuming the requirement that the marriage not be consummated makes this no longer an option…"

Mortification burst over her, forcing her to lower her lashes. Having her sexuality discussed in this room full of seething testosterone was not at all what she wanted.

"What about something to do with coercion?" Aiden asked.

That brought Christina's head up. Surely, he wasn't inferring that she— But then he continued. "After all, James coerced me into this. Even though Christina volunteered, she was simply trying to help me, to help Lily. We'll go at it from that angle."

She should thank him for thinking of her. If only he wasn't fighting for something she wasn't sure she wanted.

"It doesn't matter," Canton broke in. "James wanted everything to continue as is. If you'll just allow me to continue—"

"Spit it out," Aiden demanded, his voice sounding like a growl.

Jacob and Luke nodded their agreement. Christina remained silent. She wanted nothing from this will. Nothing except to be left alone to care for her friend. If deep down she had hoped to have a chance to hold on to Aiden just a little bit longer, then she'd bury it under the shame of his abandonment and pretend it never existed.

"James changed his will after Aiden's return and his subsequent marriage."

Christina didn't turn to look as Aiden mumbled curses under his breath. Luke's sigh was an indication that all the men realized this probably wasn't a good thing.

"He wished the marriage—and your presence— to continue the full year. He also expressed his certainty that you would disregard his instructions should he die."

Christina's stomach twisted, forcing bile up the back of her throat. James had known Aiden all too well.

"So what's the threat this time?" Aiden asked, exasperation tightening his voice. "He can no longer use Mother as leverage. Between us grandsons, money isn't an issue. So what is it now?"

Canton's grin was reminiscent of the man Christina had both feared and loathed while he was alive. She had a notion those feelings were about to kick back into gear.

"Who said Lily was out of the picture?" he asked.

Christina gasped, jerking forward as pain shot through her. She barely noticed the warmth of Luke's hand against the small of her back. Her entire focus was on the weasel behind the desk. "What are you saying?" she moaned.

"I'm saying you will stay here and take care of Lily, and Aiden will stay to take care of the town. Just as James wanted."

That should have made her feel better, but it didn't. "Why?"

"Because Lily's guardianship now reverts to me. As does control of all Blackstone funding."

Curses rolled from the men around her as they jumped

to their feet, but Christina remained frozen on the sofa. Her breath stuck in her throat so long she thought her chest would explode. Fear let loose like a runaway train—for Lily, for her future....

But a small part of her brain—the part she refused to acknowledge—whispered, *He can't leave just yet...*

"Everything will remain as is, for as long as Mr. Blackstone wished. At the end of the year, all inheritances will be dispersed and Lily's guardianship will revert to Jacob."

That was very little comfort to Christina. A lot could happen before the end of that year.

Aiden stepped forward beside her, staring Canton down as if he could force his surrender with a singular glare. "What reason could you possibly have for controlling a woman who can't defend herself, keeping her from her family and threatening her health. Much less threatening the demise of an entire town's way of life?"

"You can't get away with this," Jacob added. "When it comes to protecting our mother, we won't hold back. We'll find a way to stop you."

"According to this will," Canton said, shaking the papers in his hands, "I can. You can fight it, but again, it will take time. More time than the year in which Aiden and Christina are to carry out the conditions. If they stick to James's instructions, your mother will be perfectly safe from me."

"Wait," Christina whispered, pulling to her feet. "Did you say all inheritances?"

Canton's gaze leveled on her once more. "Yes."

"Since they're present, I assume Marie and Nolen receive something, as well? You're saying they have to wait until we fulfill these requirements before you will give them their portions?"

"It isn't me, my dear. It's the will. If his wishes are not carried out, James left instructions for his assets to be liquidated, Lily to be moved and no one to receive anything further. Guardianship will eventually go to Jacob, but the only inheritance will go to the university. The mill will shut down completely."

No, no, no. "That inheritance is Marie's and Nolen's retirement," she said. After everything they'd been through with James, they more than deserved the means to live out their lives comfortably. Not struggle day in and day out on a lifetime of counting pennies.

So instead of lowering the bar with his death, James had upped the ante. He was threatening not just his daughter and the town, but anyone who meant anything to Christina. Too bad he wasn't here for her to take apart piece by piece.

Christina forced herself to speak, though the words would barely move past the tight muscles in her throat. "So if we don't do this, everyone loses? You're okay with carrying out those instructions?"

Canton inclined his head in that condescending way of his. "I am."

The horror of what he was saying sank through the fog in Christina's brain. "Why?" she murmured.

"Money." Aiden spat the word out in disgust. "Why else? Did he make it worth your while, Canton?"

Once more the weasel gave that regal nod. "Very much so. But as James Blackstone was my client, I am obligated to honor his wishes."

"I'll bet," Luke said.

Canton's face took on a stony edge. "Again, you are welcome to bring in lawyers, but it will take time. Better to just continue as planned."

Seeing Aiden practically vibrating with anger, Christina figured the plans had pretty much been blown to hell and back.

Aiden could have done without dinner at Black Hills's local country club, where the elite of the entire northern county considered it a privilege to be seen. Give him a sophisticated restaurant in New York any day. This was simply people eating overpriced food for the chance to be ogled.

Right now, he preferred solitude.

But his brothers had insisted on a nice dinner before they both left. Luke would be away for quite a while as he got ready for racing season. Jacob was headed out to start preparations for moving back home. It would take him some time, but the move was a definite. The will said nothing about Aiden hiring someone to run the plant, so he was still abiding by the letter of the law.

James's law. The cause of all the tension, especially between him and Christina. The wife he'd tried at the first opportunity to get rid of after persuading her to have sex with him.

Brilliant.

How could one woman make him feel so out of control and alert at the same time? He was always trying to guess what she'd do next—when she wasn't driving him crazy with desire. Amazing. Christina was everything *but* amazed by him. They'd gone back to avoiding being in the same room except for meals, where Nolen kept a close eye on Aiden.

He was surprised Luke had been able to convince her to come with them. Yet here she was, seated on his left between him and Luke around the circular table.

The rich gold of the walls and amber lighting highlighted the dark brown color of her hair and emphasized the creaminess of her skin and the shadow along the neck he'd been itching to explore for days. He kept glancing her way, which was dangerous. He knew that. Still, he couldn't stop.

Which was how he noticed the light in her eyes as she talked.

"Y'all remember how much fun the fair was growing

up? At least, I really enjoyed the few times I got to go. And the kids at school always made a big deal about it. I think it's a great idea."

Wait. "What?" Aiden asked.

"Where have you been, dude?" Luke ragged him.

Mooning over a woman. "Just thinking about some work stuff. What's going on?"

Jacob chimed in. "Christina has a great idea for building morale in the community. You know, considering all the changes and stuff going on, it might help to foster some goodwill. Show everyone you aren't the same as old Scrooge, I mean, James."

Aiden glanced toward his wife with a raised brow, causing her to shrug with a sheepish grin. "Women think about these things," she said. "I was just considering how to signal to the community that you are trying to keep everything together, bolster sales and stuff, instead of prepping the mill to sell. It would be nice to do something totally unrelated to the mill that would just be a nice gesture for the community."

Aiden leaned back in his chair. As an art dealer with his own company, he tended to work alone more often than not. He wasn't really familiar with fostering a community's goodwill; the extent of his charity thus far had been monetary contributions. But he could see her point, and Christina knew these people a lot better than he did. "So the idea is…"

"We could bring in a fair. Do a bunch of competitions with prizes, games, food, hire a carnival with good rides. We could even use the proceeds to sponsor something like new equipment for the playground downtown."

As the others bounced ideas around, Aiden couldn't take his eyes off Christina's excited expression. It struck him hard that this woman had a seriously underused talent. He'd never known someone who could bring people together so easily and created a bond that snapped into place as seamlessly as LEGO pieces. Yet she continually remained on the outside of the circle.

Even though he wanted to resist, his brain couldn't stop asking why.

Watching her so closely allowed him to catch the brief grimace that twisted her lips before her face resettled into the smooth calm that she constantly showed the world. He wondered what she was hiding beneath the surface. For once, he was going to find out.

"What's the problem?" he asked.

She glanced around the table, then back at him. "What do you mean?" she asked when she realized he was talking to her.

Luke and Jacob tuned in, but Aiden ignored them. "I mean, why did you frown like that? What's the matter?"

He could see the why-do-you-care expression form as she took a bite of her bread. Her standoffishness was getting old, even though the fault lay solely with him. He leaned closer. "It's not nice to make me drag it out of you. Just tell me."

Her pout was quickly squashed. *Good girl.* Because he wasn't afraid to make a spectacle of himself. These people meant nothing to him, but he and Christina would be spending a lot of time together—another ten months, as a matter of fact. He wasn't going to be miserable the whole time, and he didn't want her to be, either.

"My father is sitting near the French doors," she said with a tilt of her head.

Luke scoffed. "He barely qualifies for the title."

"How would you know?" Aiden asked.

Luke sized him up for long moments, while Jacob simply watched the play from the sidelines. Finally, Luke spoke, "I actually talk to her, that's how. Conversations have a way of revealing things like that."

Ouch. His brother had been a bit touchy since the reading. Apparently, the aggravation ran a bit deeper than worry over his new race car. But it couldn't compare to Aiden's being schooled in front of the woman he—wanted. A lot.

Aiden chose to ignore his brother. "Do you talk to your family at all, Christina?" he asked.

Her shrug gave the impression that she didn't care, but the teeth steadying her lower lip spoke otherwise. "Not if I can help it. But that's okay. They aren't much on talking to me, either. When they do, it's more *at* me than anything else."

Aiden looked over and noted that the woman seated at the table with Christina's father was young enough to be her sister. Which reminded him to ask, "What about your mom?"

"I talk to her more often, usually when she calls."

"To check on you?"

"Not really."

Not wanting this to become a grill session, but anxious to keep her talking, Aiden asked quietly, "Then what for?"

Christina was silent for too long. Aiden was on the verge of pushing when Luke answered, instead. "She wants money."

Huh? "I thought your parents had money," Aiden said.

He should be irritated at her for rolling her eyes, but it was kind of cute. "My dad does. My mom falls into the genteel poverty category."

"Ah, she's always calling for a handout."

"No," she said, drawing the word out. "After the first year of my stint with Lily, she learned I meant no when I said it. I'm not even really sure why she bothers calling anymore." She crumpled the last of her bread onto her plate, tearing tiny pieces off at a time.

"They divorced when you were…"

"Eight. The split between them was ugly. Very ugly."

Christina shuddered over memories he could only imagine. "Of course, my mother gave him a lot of ammunition to work with. Affairs. Alcohol abuse. That sort of thing."

"And he left you with her?" Aiden couldn't imagine leaving a child of his in that type of situation. Apparently, James had been a walk in the park compared to Christina's childhood.

"Wealthy businessmen have a lot more on their minds than child rearing, or so he said."

That must have hurt. Especially to a girl of eight.

"He basically paid Mother off to take me, giving her a generous amount of child support, though he stinted on the alimony in view of her numerous affairs. That didn't stop her from asking for more, telling him I needed uniforms or new books for school, dental work, anything to con more money out of him. Sometimes she made stuff up, just to see if it would work."

He eyed the polished man across the room. "Did it?"

"Not as often as she would have liked. Which made me more trouble than I was worth. Not a lot has changed since then, for either of them." Christina moved her salad around on her plate. "Can we talk about something else, please?"

As the last of her earlier excitement faded from her eyes, Aiden's guilt kicked in. People looking in from the outside probably saw her as privileged. He saw a hard childhood, a complicated life, and he hadn't made it any easier. "How does she support herself without your income now?"

"Same way she did then. Always on the hunt for some wealthy man to support her bad habits. There have been quite a few, even another ex-husband, though it's getting hard as she ages. I get calls for money every couple of months. Honestly, enough of my expenses are paid at Blackstone Manor that I have the extra money to spend on her, but…"

"It would just be wasted."

She nodded. "Exactly. Instead, I've opened a money market account that I add to every month. Mother doesn't even realize she has a retirement fund, without any of the work to go along with it."

Acting on an unexpected desire, Aiden stretched his hand across the space between them. He didn't hold Christina's hand, but simply stroked his fingers along the back of it, once again savoring the smooth feel of her skin.

She shifted, uncomfortable with either the conversation or his touch. Christina didn't talk about herself much. In all actuality, she didn't put herself forward a great deal, only when she was advocating on behalf of someone else. Though she often complicated his own plans, forcing him to see all sides of the story, he couldn't help but admire her motives.

The only other truly selfless woman he'd known had been his mother.

Aiden couldn't help but compare Christina's childhood to his own, at least before they'd come to live at Blackstone Manor. His father had been an attentive man, balancing his work as a professor of business management with an active family life. He'd generously lavished attention on his wife and children, which had made the move to the manor that much more unpleasant. After that, his father's time had run out. He'd come home from work late every night exhausted, and left early in the morning before the boys were out of bed. Aiden had missed him with an ache that had been unbearable sometimes. Unfortunately, his mother had borne the brunt of his bid for more attention. Something he deeply regretted now.

He stared at the woman beside him, one who seemed so together and on top of things, and wondered what she had done to gain attention as a teenager. And instead of making those years easier, Aiden had tried to run her off from the only home she'd been able to create. Boy, he was a bastard.

She had taken her life in a much healthier direction than a lot of girls in her situation would have. It was just one more thing to admire her for; if only it didn't make him feel like even more of a screwup. No amount of success in his work had ever made that feeling go away.

Which meant keeping his distance from her was all that much more essential. Developing any kind of relationship with her was crazy, but the simple truth was he couldn't stay away. Deep down, he didn't want to. He knew himself well enough to realize he couldn't keep his hands to himself for the next ten months.

The question was, what should he do about it?

Twelve

Christina didn't pull her hand back as quickly as she should have, but knowing that simple touch was the only thing she'd ever have from Aiden made it hard. Still, watching her father walk toward her table evoked more emotions than she could handle. Nerves and resignation churned in her stomach, not mixing well with what she'd had for dinner.

How, after all these years, could the man who had biologically sired her still make her want to shrivel up into a tiny ball to escape his notice?

George Reece paused next to their table, drawing all eyes to him. His presence was commanding, much the same way as James's. Money, self-confidence and a hard personality would do that for a man.

Christina's brother brought up the rear. His height and thick, dark hair matching his father's, Chad was a couple of years younger than she was, but according to George, he might as well have been an only child. He didn't have his father's presence, instead putting off the I-don't-care vibes of a young man with no responsibilities and even less drive. His gaze flickered around the table, before sliding away to assess if any of his peers were in the dining room.

Rounding out the trio was Tina, Christina's stepmother. Or rather, the woman her father had married. After all, she was only twenty-eight to Christina's twenty-six. With her

stereotypical big blond hair and tan, she had the lithe figure of a woman who worked hard on her body, the blank
stare of a woman who didn't care about her brains and the
fake boobs to crown her the ultimate trophy wife.

George never had liked 'em smart.

His gaze roamed the table before coming to rest on
Christina. "Well, girl, aren't you going to introduce me?"

Her muscles jerked, instinct urging her to hop to her
feet and make introductions, but she resisted. Instead, she
rose with carefully controlled grace and inclined her head.
"Daddy. How are you?"

Approval drifted through his distinctive dark eyes, so
like her own. She wished she felt some positive emotion,
but truthfully, she never had. Self-preservation would do
that to a girl.

"I heard through the grapevine you've been busy."

But he couldn't be bothered to call and find out for sure,
could he?

Tina giggled.

Aiden stood as well, hopefully distracting everyone from
Christina's reddening cheeks. His full height only topped
her father's by an inch, but to Christina it could have been
a foot. Her father's condescending glare lost a little power
when he had to look up. "I apologize for not recognizing
you, Mr. Reece. It's been a long time," Aiden said.

"I'm sure living in New York for so long has dimmed
your hometown memory," George said, though his tone
gave the impression he didn't understand how anyone could
forget him. "Luke, Jacob." He nodded to each man in turn.

Finally, he zeroed back in on Christina. "It would have
been customary to invite us to the wedding. Especially
when you were marrying a Blackstone. Ungracious of you."

Behind her father, Chad smirked. Her father enjoyed his
social position. It never occurred to her that her marriage
would be the one thing guaranteed to garner his approval.

Jacob and Luke rose as one, but Aiden spoke before they could. "Considering my grandfather's health, we thought it prudent to keep the ceremony *very* private."

"Yeah," Luke drawled. "I didn't even know about it until it was time to cut the cake."

Christina flushed as the memory flooded over her, despite Luke's surreptitious wink.

George didn't acknowledge the men's excuses, but they seemed to put him in a better mood. "It's about time you started making choices worthy of your heritage. Acting like the lady you should be, instead of somebody's servant."

Tina couldn't help but add her two cents. "Well, it did help her snare a rich husband."

Luke mumbled something that sounded suspiciously like "You outta know," distracting Christina from the coming lecture. When he could be bothered, her father had criticized everything from her clothes to her reading material since she was born. Her nursing career was a particular sore spot.

Even more humiliating was that this should happen here, in front of Aiden. But in the same way it was hard to warn a speeding train of an impending collision, she saw no way to stop the man determined to see the worst in her.

"Christina's not a servant. She's based her career on helping those in need. But I'm guessing you're not fond of doing unto others." Jacob drawled. She thought he was echoing her thoughts, then realized he was referring to her father's last statement.

"Why should I be?" George asked. "What good does it do me?"

She could almost feel the men jerk in surprise. Not her. She knew her father better than he probably realized. He was all about getting ahead, and dropping everything that didn't help him do that by the wayside. Like the child he hadn't wanted.

Aiden let her father's comment slide. "Well, her care has certainly kept our mother alive all these years. We're grateful to Christina for that."

She managed a weak smile, then chastised herself for glancing at her father for his reaction.

"And again I ask, what good has that done her?" George didn't slow down even though Christina could feel anger spark in the men around the table. "Years spent at an invalid's bedside, when she could have been earning her place in South Carolina society. But that's where she'll be in the end, thanks to her bloodline and now her marriage. In time, people will forget her common laborer background and see her as they should, as the wife of the Blackstone heir."

Christina gasped, his expectations cutting through the hard-earned self-respect of taking care of herself and others since college.

Before she could gather herself, Aiden was around the table and towering over her father. "All that hard work did gain her something—a family that cares about her, unlike the people who donated the sperm and the egg. You aren't a father—it's a father's job to protect his children, not tear them down."

Unused to being dominated, George opened his mouth. But Aiden didn't give him a chance to speak. His mouth split into a predatory grin as he stared her father down. "So run on about your business. Christina *is* well taken care of, all without any effort on your part. And don't expect any invitations to the manor. We prefer to keep our environment...pleasant."

The roar in her ears covered up George's response, though it must have been weak considering the grins shared between the brothers. Aiden had defended her with a knight's loyalty. As the Blackstone men surrounded her, tears welled for the first time since she'd seen her father across the room.

Her defenders. Her protectors. Her comrades. Finally, family had found her.

* * *

Christina flopped onto her empty bed, stretching out as far as her body would let her. Nicole had a few night shifts for the next few days, allowing Christina the luxury of sleeping uninterrupted. She planned to enjoy it, no matter how lonely it might be. Curling over onto her side, she lay quietly in the glow of her bedside lamp. Though her mind craved rest, her body wouldn't shut down, even after the hot bath she'd taken.

The gentle drip of the soft rain outside should have calmed her, but instead, her mind spun. She wasn't even sure what it was about Aiden that made her crave him so much. Those rare times when they worked together to solve a problem made her mind sing. His confession about his father and his attempt at reaching his mother made her heart ache. Even arguing with him had her adrenaline humming. More than anything, his smile, his touch, made her heart come alive. And his defense of her against her father's criticism—she'd never forget it.

Thoughts of him were always there, like a lingering presence at the back of her mind. But she'd distracted herself all afternoon by planning for the upcoming fair. She'd roped in some women to help her, made tons of phone calls, lists and plans, and then saw Jacob and Luke to the door when Aiden took them to the airport.

He'd watched her all day, his gaze stroking her body as if his hands wished to do the same. He didn't touch her, and he hadn't since that last time. Yet she'd known his focus on her was carnal. He wanted her. Her body knew it and that knowledge left her tingly and aching. What would she do if he joined her in this bed once more, if he reached out for her?

The response of her body was answer enough. If he came to her, she would take whatever he was willing to give. He was an addiction. As much as she wished he could love her, she would settle for less, just to have him one more time.

Sad as that might be, it was the truth.

From the time she was young, she'd dreamed of having someone who would want her for herself. Not because she fulfilled a role as their daughter. Not because of the money she could provide. Not because of the services she had to offer. Someone who wanted Christina, well, just because.

Aiden wanted her for a lot of reasons. But when he held her in his arms, she *felt* as if he wanted her for herself. She simply wanted to feel that one more time. There were too many reasons why she couldn't have him forever.

A knock sounded on the door to the outer hallway. Christina stared at it for a moment, a feeling of inevitability settling over her. Just as she rose up on her elbows, the door opened. Aiden stepped inside, then closed the door with a firm click.

His posture looked relaxed, his unbuttoned dress shirt showcasing the tight muscles along his abdomen and the rise and fall of his chest from his rapid breathing. Then he stalked forward, one slow step at a time. His hooded eyes bored into her, leaving her breathless and shaking.

"What are you doing here?" she asked, jumping to her feet.

"Don't you know?"

Forcing herself to push out her arm, she stopped him at arm's length. "Aiden, we need to talk about this. I can't—" she swallowed hard "—I can't go back and forth. I need to know what we're doing here."

Reaching out, he brushed her thick hair behind her ear, caressing his finger over the skin. A shiver worked its way over her neck and down her arms.

"I'm not playing games, Christina. We both want each other. I, for one, cannot ignore it anymore."

She stared at his face, straining to see something, some

answer to what was driving his passion. "So I'm just convenient. Is that it?"

"Far from it, sweetheart. The way you make me feel isn't convenient at all."

His glittering black eyes didn't falter. Christina had a choice: she could take a risk or play it safe. With slow steps, she skirted the bed until she stood before him. Lifting to her tiptoes, she brushed her lips across his. Her sighing breath mingled with his.

"I want you, Aiden," she whispered, tucking her fear deep down inside where no one could see. Not even her.

"And I want you, Christina. More than I ever thought possible." He gently pushed her back onto the cool cotton of the comforter and crouched over her. "Remember, we're in this together."

She was half-prepared for him to change his mind and pull away. He always pulled back from her, always found a way to distance himself. He would this time, too, somehow. But she was done holding back.

"Please," she whispered, giving herself permission to reach for him. "You are what I need."

With a growl, he drove forward, taking her mouth once more, sinking his tongue deep. He went from zero to sixty in a few seconds, as if he'd thrown off restraint along with his shirt. She could fight no more. Need was all-consuming. She had to have him, no matter what the aftermath.

Aiden devoured her mouth with skill and devastation. First he rimmed her lips with his tongue, then delved deep to explore. He didn't rush like the last time they were together. Instead, he lingered at her mouth, his body crowding over hers, his fists digging into the mattress on each side of her head. Like a gentle trap, his hold left her little freedom, but all the sustenance her soul could possibly need.

He nibbled her lower lip, moaning low in his throat. Christina's entire body came to attention, instantly taut from her chest to the soles of her feet. The ache to once more feel his hands on her skin was overwhelming.

She returned his kiss with all the intensity building inside her. When that wasn't enough, she arched her back, her body meeting his inch for inch. After long minutes he pulled back until they were barely touching, yet close enough for their breath to mingle.

"I'm going to take you so, so slow, Christina, until I touch every part of you." His breath brushed along her cheek. Though fear lingered, she forced herself to look him in the eye. She found his complete and total focus on her, as if whatever barrier he'd been holding up between them had been shattered.

Excitement locked her breath in her throat for a moment, then it rushed back as her barriers completely collapsed. With both hands, she tunneled into his thick, brown hair and pulled his mouth back down to hers. If this was the only place he would touch her, that's what she would take.

Giving in to her demands, Aiden's hands glided along her bare arms, savoring her skin in long strokes. He touched her over and over, as if he couldn't get enough. Moving his hands up and along her neck to cup her jaw, he cradled her face once more for his kiss.

"I have to feel you, Christina. I have to feel more of you," he said, reaching for the hem of her tank top. Impatient, he pulled it over her head in one swipe, leaving her torso naked beneath his hot stare. She stretched, shamelessly offering herself to him, desperate for his touch.

He gave it to her. His large hands cupped and shaped her breasts, teasing her nipples unmercifully. Stroking from her ribs up to the tips, she felt them tighten just for him. He rewarded her with licks and gentle bites until she couldn't hold back the cries building in her throat. She craved warm skin and soft hair. Every touch filled the empty well inside her, the space that had been abandoned for so very long. Her hands weren't enough. With no more inhibitions, she circled his lower back with her legs, trying to pull him down.

As if their minds were linked, he bent to rub his bare chest along hers. She cried out in pleasure, arching in an attempt to keep contact with as much of him as possible. Her hands clutched at his back, savoring the feel of flexing muscles and hard ribs.

With a growl, he stood. His gaze held hers as his hands moved to the zipper of his pants. She wanted to look as he revealed himself, eager to enjoy his body in all its glory, but she couldn't tear her gaze from his. All that intensity, all that focus, for her.

Rising to her knees, she sealed her mouth once more to his. He pulled her close while his hot hands caressed her back, traveling down to slip beneath the waistband of her pajama pants. The feel of him cupping and shaping her melted her all the way to her core. Before there had been fire; now she was an inferno.

With a soft push, he tossed her back onto the bed and stripped off her pants. Her thighs spread wide, eager for attention. She thought he would enter her quickly, but that would have been too easy. Bending at the waist, he once more buried his face against her core to wreak havoc.

Obliterating what little control she had left.

Tongue and fingers played with devastating skill, driving her to the brink before Aiden pulled back. Her face burned as he reached for the little foil packet from his pants pocket, sheathing himself with ease.

No family, no matter how much she might dream.

Flexing his leanly muscled arms, he hooked his hands underneath her knees and pulled, dragging her to the edge of the bed, positioning her perfectly for his entry. His strength left her at once vulnerable and powerful. His urgency spoke of a desperate need. For her. For Christina. For the satisfaction her body could bring him.

A satisfaction she was more than willing to give.

For once uninhibited, she opened her legs wide, bending her knees to rest her heels on the edge of the bed. He leaned forward, guiding his hardness to her liquid heat. Eager, she lifted her hips, anxious for that first touch.

It came too soon and not soon enough. He hissed as his flesh met hers, clenching his teeth. He pushed slowly inside, an inch in, then out again. Feeling every bit of pressure and fullness as he stretched her, Christina struggled to remain still. She wanted to feel every inch. But her core wouldn't listen. Her inner muscles clenched around his invading length, stroking it with welcome.

Aiden's breath changed. He panted out her name, lungs struggling to keep up. Christina's control shattered. Within minutes, her head thrashed from side to side, her hands grasping the sheets beneath her.

Aiden's lower body rocketed into overdrive, thrusting heavily within her, setting off explosion after explosion as sensation built to a fever pitch. All the while his lips clung to her nipples, multiplying the riot along her nerves a thousandfold.

Within seconds, her orgasm burst through her, captivating her body and roaring through her mind. His hands clamped onto her shoulders and he buried himself as far as he could, then froze with an expression of stunned ecstasy. His groan drowned out her heartbeat as she savored every breath, every touch.

Pride and satisfaction drifted through her euphoric state. Aiden collapsed across her stomach. Her fingers trailed along the heaving muscles of his back as she counted his heartbeats. Here was what she had craved for so long: this man, this moment, this passion.

All had been more than she'd ever hoped for.

Thirteen

Aiden lay spooned around Christina's back. He had never been the cuddling type. But he'd been drawn here with no other explanation than that…it felt right. The whole time they'd lain together, his hands had been moving like a slow, lazy river, stroking over whatever skin was within reach— her arms, back, hips, thighs, even demanding access to her breasts and stomach. He couldn't stop.

Beneath his touch, a fine tremble ran through Christina. Like a purring kitten, her body showed its appreciation, maybe even without her permission.

He shouldn't be lying here with her. Hell, he should never have come to her room. There was a certain practicality in his argument, but the bare truth? He couldn't control himself. He'd never run into that with another woman. He'd always been able to walk away the day after. But now that he'd told himself he could have her, there was no going back. Despite the circumstances, he couldn't wait to have her *again*.

Her softly spoken words distracted him from the surges of lust in his veins.

"What changed your mind?" she asked.

"About what?" The deep notes of satisfaction in his voice were unfamiliar.

"About being with me?"

He could tell from her hesitation that she didn't really

want to pursue this line of conversation, so he admired her for sticking to her guns. If they were going to be intimate with each other, she deserved to know some of what he was thinking. Better to know the why of it and that it would end, than to get her heart all tangled up in something that wouldn't last.

He sighed, his long fingers squeezing her hip before moving up to rest at her waist. "Haven't you learned anything about me yet, Christina?"

"What do you mean?" she asked, stiffening against him.

Not that he blamed her. "I'm one of those unpredictable types who flies off the handle and lives to regret it later." Like the first time they'd been together. "What happened between us last time wasn't your fault and wasn't my fault. It was a product of this attraction between us."

As if eager to demonstrate, his hips surged against her, making very clear that the attraction he referred to hadn't diminished in the slightest. If anything, he felt hungrier than he had half an hour ago.

Lifting up, he let her fall to her back so that he crouched over her upper body. She bravely met his gaze, turbulent eyes looking both afraid and exhilarated. Aiden didn't do things by half measures. He could be controlled, as in his dealings with Balcher, but he wouldn't apologize for the passions constantly churning beneath the surface, just waiting for an opening to burst free.

"We're going to be here, in this house, together, for a while yet. Despite how this all came about, we have the same goals—to take care of Lily and make sure the mill remains viable. There's no way I can ignore the way I feel around you in the meantime. So unless you tell me this isn't what you want, I think we should just accept this as a connection we both can benefit from in a bad situation."

Breath catching in her throat, Christina went very still for long moments. Aiden was being honest, something that wasn't always appreciated. They were both eager to protect themselves, but there was no reason why they couldn't enjoy the desire between them while it lasted.

He would just have to keep it from going any deeper than that.

Christina jerked awake from a deep sleep, her heart racing, body poised to run. The suspicion that she'd forgotten something important pounded through her brain. What was it? What was the matter?

She glanced toward the clock, only to find the view blocked by a bare chest with a sprinkling of hair. As she watched, Aiden rolled to his side, his dark eyes blinking languidly in her direction. "Morning, beautiful," he murmured.

Was it the sleep-roughened voice or the morning stubble that melted her all the way to her core? Or simply the fact that it was morning and he was still within touching distance? What a way to wake up—

Morning! Sitting up, Christina spied the late hour on the bedside clock and shot out of bed.

"Christina, where are you going?"

"I'm late," she said as she closed herself in the bathroom. She didn't allow herself more than a quick swipe of the brush through her hair and use of her toothbrush before she was back out again.

Aiden had migrated to the edge of the bed as she swept past. She thought he would ignore her in favor of lying back down. Instead, he followed her to the dressing room. Besides a cabinet of gowns and bedding for Lily, the dressing room now served as Christina's closet. She pulled out a set of scrubs and struggled not to blush as she changed her panties.

"I can't believe I slept so late," she said, trying to take the focus off what she was doing. Which was very difficult, considering she'd never had a man watch her dress, much less one who stared with the intensity of a painter memorizing her curves.

"It isn't surprising," Aiden said. Just as she turned to ask why, he teased, "After all, I did keep you up pretty late."

That was an understatement. He'd come to her room after ten last night, and had woken her up twice more after they'd turned out the lights. Not that his insatiability bothered her. She'd been willing and just as eager.

No, every bit of tiredness was worth the incredible experience of last night. Except now her blush suffused not only her cheeks but her entire body, as well. But really, was there any point in being shy about it? What had happened between them in her bed wasn't something she'd willingly give up.

So she chose to tease back, instead. "And I'm pretty sure you aren't sorry in the least," she said with a saucy grin. "No matter that I won't be good for much today."

"Nope," he conceded, but his smile faded as she rushed to the opposite door.

She paused with her hand on the knob and glanced at him over her shoulder. The sadness creeping over his grin made her ache. To her knowledge, he hadn't been to see his mother since that midnight conversation she'd overheard, but she couldn't force him. He had to make this decision for himself. "I have to go to work," she said.

He nodded, smile long gone. She forced herself to turn away, not to linger or reach out to him in any way. But the disappearance of their earlier connection still hurt.

When Christina entered Lily's suite, Nicole glanced up from where she was packing her books. "I was just coming to knock on your door," she said.

Thank goodness she hadn't planned to just walk in like usual. Nicole always had been a smart girl. "Sorry I'm running late. Ready for your quiz today?"

"As ready as I can be…" Nicole's voice and gaze trailed away, causing Christina to glance behind her.

Aiden stood in the doorway to the dressing room, having pulled on his khaki pants, but nothing else.

Turning back, Christina found a big smile plastered on Nicole's face and an approving look in her eyes. Again with the damn blush! Though Nicole would have heard through the grapevine about Aiden's mattress-moving strategy, Christina wasn't used to parading her love life in front of others.

"Thank you, Nicole," Christina said, her voice quieting. The other woman left the room as Christina turned to the bed, going through her usual motions of checking Lily's pulse and temperature.

She was aware of Aiden as he came into the bedroom and leaned against one of the chairs near the doorway. The same chair he'd sat in before. But she had a feeling he wouldn't let his guard down enough to do so today.

She studied him through her lashes as she talked to Lily in a low, soothing tone.

"You doing okay this morning, sweetie? Nicole takes good care of you, doesn't she?"

Aiden maintained his distance, his posture closed off, arms crossed over his chest. The sunlight filtering through the curtains glinted off the spiky points in his chestnut hair, but didn't illuminate his eyes. She tried not to notice the tight strength of his thighs as he stood there.

His complete lack of movement amazed her. He didn't so much as fidget. Ordinarily, his shut-down expression might have indicated disgust or lack of caring, but she suspected it was more a product of caring too much.

It hurt him to see his mother like this.

Which was the very reason he'd avoided this room. She'd seen it so often, she wished she could tell him he wasn't the only one, but didn't want to risk scaring him off by getting too deep. She settled for, "You haven't spent much time in a sickroom."

His eyes widened slightly before his face resumed an emotionless mask. "Does it show?"

Sighing, she sank into her chair on the opposite side of the bed. Why had she thought he would make this easy on either of them?

She smiled down at Lily, the woman who'd become a surrogate mother to her before the older woman's accident. Her heart ached with the guilt of her involvement. "It's often hard for family and friends in situations like this. Not only does it hurt to see her sick and unresponsive, but it is an awkward situation."

She cast a tentative smile in his direction, wanting to connect, but fearful of rejection. She wasn't going to mind her own business, even if he was Lily's son. Lily had talked so much about him—his drive to succeed, his interest in art, his independence, his loneliness. She had truly loved him.

And now he was Christina's husband. She needed him more than he'd ever understand.

"It's much easier for nurses, who have charts to check, exercises to perform and chores like dressing and bathing. We have a purpose, a job to do. We can be—" she swallowed "—useful to both the patient and their families."

And useful she'd proven to be, as always. Far more so than she'd ever intended, despite her resolve never to travel that path again. She'd been useful to her mother for a while. James, too. Her father had rejected her because she was not of use to him. Which side would Aiden fall on?

"How long have you worked here?" Aiden asked, relaxing enough to stroll to the window and glance out. Was he remembering this room, the view from his childhood years here?

She had continued to spend time with Lily during high school and university, eager to have someone in her life who cared whether she succeeded or failed. "Almost five years." Something she was very grateful for, since it also allowed her to give back to Lily after her accident. Their relationship had deepened before the stroke rendered Lily comatose. "I was here visiting Lily one day when James called me to the study. He offered to give me a job taking care of her if I would come live here with them."

"He asked you?"

"Yes." She'd been happy, but Lily had been ecstatic. Only later did she realize how tough it was being a live-in nurse of someone she loved and knowing she'd probably never recover.

Aiden went on, "You weren't looking for work?"

"My father gave me a small trust fund that helped me through college, so I hadn't planned to actively search out work until the next semester," Christina said. "My last one."

She thought she heard him mumble "Very clever," under his breath, but she kept speaking as she absently rubbed Lily's arm.

"As soon as my degree was completed, I came here to live, assisting Lily with her daily activities, exercises and stuff. The years before her stroke were good ones, despite the paralysis from the car accident."

The words seemed so mundane compared to the reality. She'd built a life here, loving Lily, Nolen, Marie, Nicole and the rest of the staff as a family. She couldn't have enjoyed them more if she'd handpicked them. Despite her awkward childhood, she finally had girlfriends who lived in town, women she could talk to on the phone and shop with. Blackstone Manor wasn't just a place she worked. It was home.

"Good years," she whispered, turning watery eyes to Lily's quiet features. Her hand shook a bit as she reached out to smooth the coverlet. The last few weeks had left her way too emotional.

Aiden surprised her by speaking from the foot of the bed. When had he moved so close?

"How can you handle seeing her like this?"

Christina turned to face him, startled by the turbulent emotions so evident after his earlier composure. So she'd guessed right. He hadn't avoided his mother because he didn't want to see her, but because he wanted it so badly. To see her as she was before the accident had changed her. He wanted to avoid the painful emotions stirring inside him.

Something she could relate to but not condone. "Because I love her."

His gaze shifted to Christina and he stared intently, as if anxious to verify her words. They were true. Even without their history, Christina would have loved Lily's peaceful acceptance of her situation, pride in her children's accomplishments and graceful offer of friendship.

Christina only wished she could have begged Lily's forgiveness before the stroke had separated them forever.

"What if it was your fault that she's lying there?" Aiden asked.

The muscles around Christina's heart squeezed down hard. She couldn't move, couldn't breathe. It was her greatest fear laid bare before her very eyes. One hard thump reverberated in her chest, then another, until everything returned to its normal pace.

But Christina would never be the same. "What do you mean?" she forced out.

His hand shook slightly as he indicated his mother in her hospital bed. "I mean this. It's all my fault."

Christina should not have been relieved.

"Why?"

"She'd come to see me because I was too selfish to bow to James's demands and come to Blackstone Manor. We'd spent a few days going to art galleries and shows. She loved the creative side of New York City." Without his seeming to notice, he'd reached down to wrap his hand casually around Lily's foot. Christina held her breath, but he continued on. "I don't know if you remember the day of her accident."

Christina remembered, all too well. The bad weather, the storm warnings.

"She assured me she wanted to get home, not wait for it to clear," Aiden said. "After all, the sun was still out." He gazed at the headboard but his eyes were fuzzy with memories. "But it got bad. Really bad. Why didn't she stop?" He squeezed his mother's foot again. "I should have made her wait. It's all my fault."

Lily's foot flexed. Her heartbeat, so steady on the monitor up until now, picked up speed. Aiden jerked back, his hands flying wide. He stared at his mother as color drained from his face.

He's gonna pass out. Christina rushed to his side. A little unsure, she snuck up against his body, leaning in to keep him steady. "It's okay, Aiden."

This close, she could see him swallow hard. "What… was…that?" he asked.

"Remember me saying that Lily's coma isn't a constant state? Coma patients can rise through the stages, then sink back down."

He nodded, even though she wasn't sure if he was comprehending.

"Sometimes it means they respond to things like weather, temperature, touch. Sometimes they can even sit up and open their eyes, but then they sink back down into the coma minutes or even hours later."

"Has Mother ever…?"

"Sat up?"

He nodded again.

"No." She stroked her hand up and down Aiden's arm. "I've often wished she would. Sometimes I think these little episodes are her way of letting me know she's still here, but in truth they may only be an involuntary physical reaction. I choose to think of them as the former, despite my nursing degree telling me it's just the body's way of releasing energy."

To her surprise, his arms went around her, hugging almost too tight. Neither of them acknowledged what prompted the embrace, just settled into it for long, long moments.

When he finally pulled away, she decided to give Aiden what he most needed right now, whether he knew it or not. Placing a hand on one sculpted arm, she whispered, "I'm sure, no matter what it is, that she'd love the fact that you are here with her. And she's perfected her listening skills over the last two years." She smiled, even though he didn't return it. But at least he didn't look whiter than white any longer. "Why don't you start with 'Hello, Mom'?"

Ignoring the ripple of his muscles under her fingertips, she let go and walked away. Gifting him with the chance to heal the rift between himself and his mother was the least she could do for both of them. She just wished she could keep him when all was said and done.

Fourteen

"We're a little too early for a harvest festival, which is what we put together for the high school last year. How can we fine-tune this summer fair, ladies?" Christina asked.

Surrounding her was a group of women who loved working together for the good of the community, and were known as the go-to choice for getting things done. They weren't from the country club like Tina's set, who simply threw money at a charity to be seen doing it. Just good women who worked hard and had fun.

"I'm so excited," Mary Creighton said, clapping her hands together like a kid. "It's been a long time since we had a *true* country fair. Or anything more than that rinky-dink carnival set up in the high school parking lot."

Jean Stanton jumped in, too. "And the fairgrounds are still in really good shape. We'll easily have enough room for anything we want to do. It'll be nice to have something to look forward to after all this—"

A hard look from the other woman had Jean closing her mouth quick, but Christina had already tuned in.

"It's okay, Mary. I need to know these things. Jean, go ahead."

Jean shrugged, setting her dangly earrings into motion. "It's just been tough with the economy and worry over what might happen to the mill after Mr. Blackstone got sick. Then our men started talking about what was going on at the mill and all…"

Christina hadn't been aware that the disturbing incidents were common knowledge. Obviously, the workers had taken note and had ideas of their own. "I know, Jean. And trust me, Aiden is working closely with Bateman to put a stop to that nonsense."

"That's good, especially after that equipment failure last week," Avery Prescott added. "Having him involved takes a load of worries off all of us about working out there. She just means it's a good time to have some fun, blow off steam…even better than a night at Lola's."

Mary's brows shot up. "Do you honestly think anything is better than a night at Lola's?"

"I can think of a few things…" Jean snuck in, leaving everyone laughing.

"Now, about the fair—" Christina prodded.

"The carnival is already contracted. A really good one, with a great safety record," Jean said. "Why not have a couple of those blow-up waterslides for the kids, too? And a watermelon-eatin' contest."

Christina hurried to scribble notes as the ideas flew fast and furious.

"A bouncy castle for the little ones."

"A cake walk."

"A petting zoo."

Mary leaned forward. "Too bad KC isn't in town. She's always good for fun adult-only ideas," she said with a waggle of her eyebrows.

"Hmmm…maybe some eye candy? I was thinking of asking Luke to come home that weekend," Christina said. "He could bring the car for display, sign autographs… I'm pretty sure both the men *and* the women will like that."

The youngest of the group now that KC Gatlin had moved away, Avery quickly chimed in. "What about a kissing booth? Would he be willing to do that? Because that man is hotter than a sidewalk in the South in July."

The other women quickly agreed. "And in his racing suit," Mary elaborated, "that man has buns tighter than—"

"Are you ladies talking about me?"

As Aiden's voice rang throughout the room, a flush encompassed Christina's entire body. The women around her froze, staring at one another with wide eyes until giggles escaped one by one. Christina tried to maintain her cool beneath Aiden's sexy grin, but her mind betrayed her with images of Aiden, naked in her bed.

Oh, that so didn't help anything.

"Aiden, these are the ladies working with me on the fair."

"Very nice," he said. "I can't thank you all enough. I know it's a lot of hard work, but we really appreciate it."

The charm came on, and every woman in the room melted into pliant goo. Even Christina. Especially Christina. He'd taken to her lessons on Southern hospitality way better than she could have imagined.

She didn't get to see this side of him often, and intense Aiden was just as attractive, but when he went out of his way to make someone feel valued, it really worked.

Determined to stop blushing, Christina tuned in to the murmurs of approval wafting his way. When her gaze followed, she found him watching her. The smoldering look in those dark eyes sent a shiver down her spine. In this room full of people, they might as well have been alone.

And deep inside, the fragile hope that he would stay burst into full bloom. She'd been fighting for so long, aching for too long… For once, the simple wish to keep someone she loved close to her overran practicality.

He turned and walked away with a small wave. Christina knew he'd be in her room when she went upstairs. Their room. She only hoped she could survive waiting that long.

Mary fanned her forty-something face. "Oh, girl. That one's a hottie, I have to say. Runs in the family. You are one lucky woman,"

Christina just sat there, her face getting warmer and warmer, while the other women enthused over her new husband's traits.

"So tall. And all that dark hair."

"And those dark eyes." Avery shivered. "So intense."

"Did you see the muscles in his arms?" Jean asked. "Talk about carry me away."

Christina refused to squirm, but something of her thoughts must have revealed themselves on her face, because the laughter tapered off.

"Oh, honey," Mary said, rushing over to pat her arm. "Are we embarrassing you?"

Christina wanted to yell *yes!* but bit her tongue, instead. Her inexperience and confusion were not their fault.

"Oh, course you are," Avery said.

Mary's concern coated her every word. "We didn't mean to, Christina. Honest."

Christina smiled her understanding. Avery put her arm around Mary and said, "We know you didn't. You just can't help it."

"Me and my big mouth, my husband always says." Mary shrugged. "I can fit both my size nines inside."

Christina smiled up at her. "No harm done."

Relief softened Mary's face. "Good."

Luckily, at that moment, the door cracked open once more, this time to reveal Nolen and a tray of goodies. He smiled over his obvious welcome and led the group to the farthest end of the room where he set up the refreshments on the table.

When she moved to join the others, Avery motioned for her to stay. "You okay, Christina?"

"Sure," Christina said. Avery had been a good friend to her. They hadn't been close when they were younger, but had reconnected when Avery had returned to town after getting her training as a physical therapist. Both were single, around the same age, with no interest in the party scene, so they had a lot in common and could talk easily about almost anything.

Avery also encouraged her to take care of herself and have fun every so often, thus the frequent invitations to Lola's.

Avery glanced at the table of women who were now moving on to other things. "That Mary is something else."

Christina nodded. "Yeah. I know she was just playing around. I just—" Christina twisted her fingers together "—haven't figured out how to respond naturally."

Avery took a drink, but her blue eyes remained calm and steady on Christina.

"I feel like everyone knows why we married and is going to judge everything I say." Christina looked to her friend for comfort.

Avery didn't disappoint. "They are not judging you," she said, reaching out to still Christina's hands with her own. "Most of them are thrilled, because the marriage gives them a sense of stability."

Christina frowned. "For their jobs?"

Avery nodded. "And for their future. Whatever the reason behind it." She leaned forward to look directly in Christina's eyes. "And that's no one's business but yours. One of the Blackstone grandsons having a permanent reason to stay here means the mill will continue to be run by the family. And if that happens through an arranged marriage—well, those have been happening all over the world since the beginning of time." She leaned back. "People in town feel they can trust the family not to abandon them, to have their best interests at heart."

Christina felt slightly sick to her stomach. If only they knew. "That's what baffles me. They don't really know Aiden at all. Not the man he is now."

Avery shook her head. "Doesn't matter. He's familiar, which is always better than the unknown."

If Christina had anything to say about it, he wouldn't disappoint. Since he possessed a mind of his own, there were no guarantees. But oh, how she wished there were. He'd worked hard for Black Hills so far. If only he would stay...

"I'm not going to pry," Avery was saying, "but you know I'm here to talk if you need me, right?"

Christina smiled. "Thank you."

Avery shrugged, then steered the conversation on to more mundane topics, helping Christina relax. This was exactly what she needed. Calm. A project to focus on. Friends to distract her.

No worries about the future. No challenging conversations. No brooding, attractive male to turn her inside out and upside down.

Life often moved in directions Christina never expected. She had spent a lifetime going to movies and restaurants alone, hanging out in coffee shops and bookstores on her days off. But as she looked around the dinner table a month later, she finally understood that she was no longer alone.

That's what family was for. And she had claimed the people around her as hers, for as long as they would let her.

"I have an idea," she said, gaining the attention of the table. Everyone was in their usual places, one end full now that Jacob had rejoined them and Luke had been able to clear a brief few days for his appearance at the fair. Nolen and Marie peeked through the door from the kitchen. "I think we should go to the fair. Together."

"Fair?" Marie said with a grin. "I haven't been to one of those since I was a kid."

Christina was glad to see some enthusiasm. "I was out there working last night and it looked so exciting. I've always wanted to go to one."

"You've never been? Not even to the county fair as a kid?" Jacob asked. "Then you definitely have to check it out. Cheap thrills for all."

Nolen, who had entered the room carrying a tray with their after-dinner coffee, threw out a word of warning. "It isn't safe for you to go alone, Miss Christina. You men should take the ladies."

Luke agreed. "I wouldn't miss it."

But there had to be a fly in the ointment. "I've got reports to finish," Aiden said, accepting his usual cup of black decaf from Nolen. "But Luke over there never met a roller coaster he didn't love."

"The Scream Machine is my favorite," Luke said, waggling his brows in a suggestive expression. "But seriously, I'd love to have some fun before I have kissing duty tomorrow night."

Aiden just snorted, which started the ball rolling.

Luke pounced. "Ah, big brother here just doesn't want everyone to know what a wuss he is."

Aiden's growl of warning was accompanied by Christina's chant, "Tell us! Tell us!"

"Luke," Aiden said, his voice deepening in warning, "I will hurt you."

A mock expression of fear covered Luke's face, drawing a laugh from the women. "In that case, I won't tell them roller coasters make you puke like a girl."

Aiden lunged for his brother, knocking him out of his chair and onto the dining room floor. The sound of male grunts and wrestling crowded out the formal atmosphere of the room. Christina stood, watching the men twist back and forth on the oriental carpet with a sort of breathless wonder. The boys had been physical as kids—at least when James hadn't been around—and Christina had watched them on her visits with a mixture of fear and fascination. She'd certainly never expected this kind of frivolity as adults. These wild antics shocked and delighted her.

Nolen calmly stepped around the writhing mass to place Christina's hot tea on the table. Jacob simply moved away, watching his brothers with an amused expression. The contrast boggled her brain. When a draw was finally called— or rather, both men claimed to have won—they stood up and continued talking as if nothing had happened. Well, that wasn't quite true.

Luke smoothed his hands over his dark blond hair then jerked his button-down shirt back into place. Aiden, on the other hand, left the evidence of their fight, for once not caring about his scuffed look. The mussed hair, red, roughened chin, and twist of his T-shirt brought naughty thoughts to Christina's mind. Her heart thudded as she imagined pulling that shirt off and adding to his breathless state.

A quick walk around the table took her to his side, where she slipped under his arm. Tucked up against him, palm resting on his heaving ribs, she met his gaze with a teasing look of her own. "We'll just check out the atmosphere. How about that?"

As Aiden's laughter faded, Christina became aware of the hushed silence in the room. She suddenly felt every inch of Aiden pressed against her, the heavy weight of his arm around her shoulders. Though the others knew they shared a bedroom, even after James's death, she and Aiden had never taken their intimate relationship farther than the privacy of that room. She knew beyond a doubt she'd inadvertently signaled to the others living in the house that their relationship was much deeper than the expected convenient marriage. Embarrassed, she drew back, only to have his arm tighten around her.

Looking up, she found his eyes trained on her face. The look he gave her wasn't angry or irritated, but still sparking with amusement and adrenaline from wrestling with his brother. He squeezed her arm. "I think that sounds like a great idea."

Her body automatically relaxed and she returned his smile with relief. Everyone else turned away, moving toward the door with excuses about preparing for their night out.

But Christina and Aiden remained locked together. She swallowed, her heart beating in excitement. Which was ridiculous. To anyone else, this would be the smallest thing imaginable, barely significant in the whole scheme of things. But her heart knew Aiden didn't make gestures, big or small, lightly. And he wasn't done amazing her tonight.

He leaned down as if to kiss her, but stopped just short of her parted lips. "So, Christina…will you go to the fair with me?"

She swallowed hard, struggling to keep her tone teasing like his. "Are you asking me on a date, Aiden?"

"I believe I am," he said, moving the final distance to brush his lips across hers. Once. Twice. "But I have to warn you that my intentions don't involve letting you kiss me good-night at the door."

Christina's heart thudded. If only this could be real. Forever. But she hid her hopes and grasped this opportunity with both hands. Because the truth was she could have now, and all the other memories they created, to keep her through the lonely days ahead.

After a lingering kiss of her own, she said, "I think I can live with that."

She held on to that mantra over the next few hours. Through dusty fairways, caramel apples and threats to ride the Sidewinder. At one point she stumbled, and Aiden steadied her at her elbow. As they continued on, his hand slid down to hers. And stayed. In the twinkle of carnival lights, Christina's heart filled with the gesture.

She wasn't a logical woman. Practicality came naturally

with her profession, but getting attached to others was in her nature. Closeness was actually a craving for her. Aiden filled that need as no one else ever had. That he was willing to do it with the whole town watching meant even more.

With one squeeze of her hand, she was lost. And happy about it.

"Mrs. Blackstone, will they make enough money for the new playground?"

Christina paused at the high-pitched voice, smiling over at Bateman and his family. She looked down at their kindergarten-aged granddaughter. "I sure hope so, sweetheart. It will be a lot of fun to have a new one, wouldn't it?"

"It sure would," Bateman's wife said. "Give me something to do with these young'uns while their mama is at work."

"I wouldn't know," Bateman said with a grin, which grew bigger when his wife swatted his arm.

"Come on, Susie Q," his wife said. "I'll let you try to win me that teddy bear."

"No, the teddy bear is for me, Grandma."

"Are you sure?" she asked as they walked away. "I could have sworn it was for me."

"This was a great idea," Bateman said. "Everyone is having fun."

Christina agreed. "And Jean is excited to keep moving the counter up on the fund-raising scoreboard. I really think the new playground will be a go."

Bateman extended his hand. "Thank you, Aiden. We needed some fun right about now. Someone to invest in our community."

Aiden shook the hand, but corrected Bateman. "It wasn't my idea. You can thank this one," he said, lifting his and Christina's clasped hands. "I just provided a little labor and encouragement."

Much to her dismay, Christina wanted to preen under

his praise. She shrugged, instead. "Getting through tough times is easier if we do it together."

Bateman smiled his approval. "As long as things stay quiet at the mill, then I think all this talk will die down. Maybe that little chat with Balcher did the trick?"

Aiden frowned into the distance. "I don't know. He doesn't seem the type to give up after a simple slap down. I feel almost as if there's a time clock ticking down to his next move."

"Let's hope not," Bateman said.

Amen. If things could stay the same, for herself and the town, Christina would be a happy woman. She used to long for something different, but now she held her breath, praying nothing would ever change. Unrealistic, but true.

Fifteen

"Are you coming inside?" Aiden asked.

Christina had been strangely silent on the way home. She got that way sometimes, and he'd learned to give her space to think. In fact, he'd taken a few unnecessary turns on the drive. The late summer night enclosed them in patchy fog, and a cool breeze blew through the open windows. It had been so long since he'd been at ease with anyone, especially in that kind of silence, that he hadn't wanted it to end.

Yet here they were, looking at each other through the open window of the truck. Luke, Jacob and Marie had long ago returned to the house, which was silent and barely lit. Aiden wanted to scoop Christina into his arms and carry her to their room, but something held him back. It was almost as if they'd moved into a new stage, and he should once again ask her permission before introducing intimacy.

Logically, he knew only his feelings had changed. But what about her?

"I'm not sure," Christina said. She still sat inside the truck, staring at him in the dark as if searching for something, but he wasn't sure what. "Aiden…"

His throat constricted in anticipation. "What is it?"

"I'm afraid."

The words barely registered. He wanted to wipe away her fear with some pat little phrases, but he couldn't. Obviously, she felt this, too. But they both had to embrace it for it to go anywhere. "I know," he finally said. "I'm a risk. But most of the things we want in life are scary. It's up to you how you deal with it."

Unwilling to coerce her decision with his presence, he turned away. The side expanse of green lawn was still damp from the dew, along with the outer ring of azalea bushes. As he approached the weeping willow tree, he heard running footsteps behind him. Turning back, he watched as Christina ran across the lawn and barreled into his chest. Together they burst through the curtain of swaying tree limbs. He wasn't quick enough to brace himself, so her momentum knocked him off balance, and they tumbled to the ground in a tangle of bodies.

But when they came to rest, Aiden found himself in a win-win situation, with Christina's toned legs straddling his thighs and her breasts snug against the hard wall of his chest.

His body surged to instant hardness, the fullness punching the back of his zipper in an attempt to reach her skin. He arched against the sensation, pressing deeper into the V of her thighs.

She glanced around them, and he let his gaze follow, then smiled. The thick fall of branches from the fifty-year-old tree isolated them from the world outside. It was a veil enclosing them in the magical discovery of each other. Christina braced her hands on his shoulders to keep him from bucking her off, but her own hips tilted, rubbing her most private of parts across his length in one long, slow slide. Aiden's heartbeat burst into overdrive.

He needed her. Now.

She crouched closer, her lips meeting his in an all-out assault. Her mouth open, tongue delving deep. He met her with everything he had to give.

He explored, tracing the inner curves of her mouth, the moist heat stirring an ache to bury himself inside her. They couldn't linger long. Aiden knew Christina's hunger grew with his own by the way she kneaded his chest and nibbled his bottom lip. Her breathy pants brushed his skin, increasing his urgency for more.

With a jerk, he had her button-down shirt open and gaping, so he could explore her smooth skin and the lace of her bra. Leaning back, she delved between her thighs for the button to his khaki pants. Her fingers fumbled for a moment before she released him, inching back so she could get the zipper down. The condom wasn't far behind.

He lay on the hard ground, barely noticing it, his hands gently squeezing her lace-covered breasts, while his wife prepared to ride him for all she was worth. And he was in heaven. The only thought pounding through his brain was a refrain of more, more, more.

She stood to shuck her own pants, and it was all he could do not to jerk her back against him. He wanted everything. More of that delightful mix of shy and brazen. More of the woman who comforted him and wasn't afraid to point out when he was wrong. More than anything, he needed her to complete his soul.

If he hadn't already been shaking, Aiden would have started. Pulling his wife back onto him, he fitted himself at her entrance and guided her down. It killed him to go slow, but suddenly, she arched her back and slid herself home.

Stealing his breath away.

Unable to sit still, to remain at her mercy, he gripped her hips, forcing her into a counterrhythm with his own body. They ground together. Aiden savored every breathless cry straining from her throat. In the darkness, he caught the swing of her hair as she moved, the curve of her jaw silhouetted against the lighter backdrop of leaves.

As he fought for completion, only one thought remained: mine.

With that, he drove himself as deeply as he could, allowing her body weight to aid him. Her cry mingled with his. Her body contracted around him as she slammed into her peak, dragging him along in the undertow.

For long moments he knew nothing but the warmth of her flesh, the pounding of his blood and the need to never let go.

Before he could stop it, his first coherent thought emerged from his hazy brain. *I don't think I can live without this.* But separation came soon enough. Christina simply slipped to the side and onto her back, her head pillowed on his biceps.

"I need to get up," she said, "but for some reason my muscles won't move anymore."

He chuckled, feeling the sound vibrate through his chest under the very spot where her hand rested. "You need to be careful. I think I could get addicted to you ending every date this way."

He heard her smile in her voice. "Oh, I think I can live with that."

And as he helped her to her feet and into her clothes, he knew that he could, too. Because damn if he wasn't in love for the first time in his miserable life.

Christina brushed the grass off her pants before pulling them back on. She should be ashamed, or embarrassed, or something...but she wasn't. Aiden didn't even give her time to put her shirt on before he was pulling her across the lawn and into the back door. She couldn't help but giggle as they raced up the stairs. "This is becoming a habit," she said breathlessly.

"This is a habit I can most definitely live with," he said with a grin.

Christina slept deep, secure in the knowledge that Aiden was curled around her, but it ended with the harsh reality of a ringing phone. She woke at the loss of warmth, her euphoria slowly fading, and listened in the predawn gloom as Aiden spoke.

"Yes?"

Amazing that his sleep-scruffy voice could still give her shivers.

"What happened?"

The murmur of the voice from the other end sounded feminine, but urgent. His assistant from New York?

"Was anything damaged?"

That had Christina sitting up.

"How many of the paintings did it ruin?"

As he listened to his assistant's answer, a thrum of anxiety hummed along Christina's nerves. What would he do? She felt selfish worrying about it, but couldn't stop the circle of thoughts in her head. What if he left and didn't come back?

Finally, he pushed the end button. The muscles of his naked back flexed as he leaned over to set the phone on the nightstand. Her mouth watered. She wanted nothing more than to trace those sleek plains with her fingertips. Last night she wouldn't have hesitated. Today everything had changed.

Aiden twisted her way. "Hey," he said, one low word reaching through her confusion. "Sorry to wake you."

"No problem." She pulled the comforter tight around her, wishing she wasn't naked. The protection of her clothes would be a big comfort right now. "What's going on?"

"Water leak at the warehouse. The alarms alerted Trisha pretty quickly, but there's still some damage. I'm gonna have to make a trip up there."

Her throat went dry. Even though she knew her fear was irrational, it still built within her. "Why? Hasn't she already got a handle on things?" At least, her report had seemed kind of lengthy.

"Do you honestly think I'm the type of guy to let someone else handle my problems for me?"

No, he wasn't. She knew better. But the thought of him leaving brought so many fears.

She didn't answer, and he didn't wait for one. He was already pulling pants and underwear out of the drawer. "I'll get a shower and pack. Find out when I can get a flight. Jacob can drive me to the airport."

"What about the mill?" she asked. Standing, she reached for a robe to wrap tight around herself.

"Jacob is catching up on things, anyway. No reason why he can't jump right in." His clipped tone told her all the questions irritated him, but she couldn't seem to stop herself.

She took a step toward him. "Don't you think you should, you know, ask Canton before you do this? What kind of provisions are there for trips? Duration, things like that."

Aiden's shoulders straightened, his jaw growing hard. "No." The single word was sharp and forceful, telling her this was the wrong question to ask. "I don't have to ask anyone for permission to do this. That business is my life and I won't lose it over some stupid game my grandfather thought he would play. Got it?"

"Even if others get hurt?"

Aiden stalked closer, his stare boring into her. "Are you insinuating that I'm not holding up my end of this bargain?"

"Are *you* insinuating that what happened here is nothing *but* a bargain?" she demanded, waving her hand over the bed.

Again, the wrong thing to say, because all emotion disappeared from Aiden's face. His guarded expression took her back to those first days together. "I'm going," he said.

With those two words, all the anger drained from Christina. Her gaze dropped to the floor at her feet. She'd blown it, letting her insecurities push Aiden farther away. Not that it mattered if he viewed their relationship as, well, not really a relationship. "Fine. I get it."

They stood in silence for long moments, but she refused to look up again, afraid that if she did, Aiden would see the devastation breaking her apart inside. He would leave, regardless. Why she'd thought she might be a reason to at least proceed with caution was ridiculous. What she wanted would never matter. It never had.

Finally, he mumbled, "I've got to shower," and stalked back through the door to the bathroom.

Wilting all over, Christina hurried to the dressing room, lingering until she heard Aiden dress and leave. An hour later, she was showered and dressed and seated at Lily's bedside, forcing herself to read aloud to her friend when she really wanted to give in to the tears threatening every second. She'd heard the house start to stir—the voices of the men as they went up and down the stairs and finally, luggage being bumped on the steps as Aiden and Nolen spoke in quiet tones.

She ignored it all. But her focus on Lily was shaky at best, especially as footsteps stopped outside the suite door. Looking up, she spied Aiden in the shadows of the hallway. Their eyes met, but she quickly looked back down to the book, unwilling to display her feelings and give him the opportunity to dismiss them.

He moved inside slowly, almost hesitant as he stepped across the threshold until he reached the foot of Lily's bed. He didn't wait for Christina to look up. He simply spoke in a tone much softer than before. "I'm leaving now. I'll call and let you know when I'll be back once I see what needs to be done."

She nodded, using every last ounce of strength to keep her expression neutral. She'd been the one who screwed up, demanding something unreasonable out of fear. But this had simply reinforced the many years life had taught her that people, relationships, weren't something she could keep. She might as well get used to it now as opposed to later.

"Do you understand what I'm saying, Christina?"

She forced her throat to work. "Sure."

"Look at me." He didn't raise his voice, but the quiet command had her aching to obey.

With a deep breath, she met his gaze with her own. "Yes?"

"I understand what's at stake here."

Do you really?

"I know the town needs me. I know Lily needs me." He paused for the span of a long breath, then continued, "I will be back. I promise."

But what about me? She ignored her thoughts and simply nodded her head.

Still, he stared. His phone started to ring, but he ignored it. With each second that ticked by, her internal shields cracked until she knew one single push would have her squalling like a baby.

"Is there anything you want to tell me, Christina?"

Her mouth opened, drawing in the breath that would push out the words *I love you.* Words he most definitely would not want to hear. So she simply shook her head.

"I'll always come back. I promise."

"Lily said she would come back, too." And she had, but the results had been disastrous. Would Aiden's return be just as devastating? Once he had another taste of New York, would he realize how much he hated being here?

"What are you talking about?" Aiden asked, his tone hardening once more. "I realize I'm responsible for her accident. That I left Mother all these years instead of setting aside my pride to see her again. I don't need you to point my responsibilities out to me, Christina."

Christina's head shot up. "That's not what I meant at all."

"Then what did you mean? Because I won't be guilted into staying here."

Once more, the ringing of the phone filled the room.

"Guess you should go, then," she said, turning back to the impersonality of the book and the quiet atmosphere of the sickroom. Things she could control. Things she couldn't screw up. She wished she could start this morning over and tuck all her ridiculous emotions inside so she couldn't complicate things.

With a curt nod, Aiden did just that, leaving her behind. Just like everyone else in her life.

Sixteen

Christina's bare feet ghosted over the back lawn, damp from the evening's dew. She couldn't stand being cooped up in the house anymore. Aiden had been gone five days. The amount of time Canton had informed Jacob he was allotted to be away. After tonight, they would be in violation of the will. Aiden hadn't contacted her personally, so she had no idea if he planned to be home by morning...or not.

She wished she had the option of escape, even if only for a few hours. Instead, she'd waited until Marie headed out for Wednesday night church. The sympathetic looks were more than she could handle.

She must have been out of her mind. Or totally blinded by the situation they'd found themselves in. How could she have been so desperate for love as to trust her heart to a man who'd told her outright he wouldn't stay?

Something inside drew her to Aiden's studio, as if by being there she could once again be close to him. She had a moment's trepidation when she reached the porch. Aiden kept the little house locked, but the single key hung with the other keys in the mudroom. She just had to be here. The door opened easily beneath her shaky fingers.

She let herself into the darkened room, reaching out her hand to feel for a light switch. Instead, her arm brushed a lamp that she suddenly remembered was sitting on the table near the door. Tracing down, she located the switch.

The soft glow that sparked to life revealed the work space Aiden prized so much.

If she were her mother, she'd put the sledgehammer she found to good use in here. She'd seen her mother pitch many a fit on her father's things before they'd divorced. She'd even keyed up his brand-new car one time. But destruction had never been Christina's thing. Guilt had. She'd spent more than her fair share of her life living with guilt.

Guilt from Lily's accident. Guilt over not preventing the stroke that had taken her beyond Christina's reach. And guilt over not being able to pull her mother from the destructive life she was determined to pursue.

Guilt was everywhere, and yet nowhere. Because it came from within Christina. Although sometimes external things fueled a person's guilt. Just as Lily's stroke had hers. Logically, as a nurse, Christina knew she had no control over that. But she'd been determined to make up for it ever since.

Hoping to distract herself from her never-ending thoughts, Christina stepped over to the shelves to check the progress of the marble pieces she'd seen on her last visit. Despite how close she'd thought they'd become over the past few months, Aiden had never invited her here. She'd trespassed only the one time, but hadn't returned. It just seemed too personal, too presumptuous on her part to invade his most private retreat, his source of solace and peace. Until he wanted her here.

Maybe he hadn't wanted her to get to know this part of him? After all, those times when he had confided in her had been times they'd connected on an intimate basis. Maybe he'd never had any intention of going any deeper than sex with her.

She wandered idly about the room, gliding her finger along his tools, resting her palms against half-finished sculptures. Until she reached the final statue in one corner. It took her a moment to make out the dark contours in the dim light. The last time she'd been here, the block of black rock streaked with gold had been carved into a slight curve along the top, and the straight edges chipped away from the sides. Now the rough stone at the bottom remained the same, but out of the rocky ground rose the silhouette of a woman. Christina. Her gaze traced the curve of her own jaw to the slight point of her chin, her abundant waves of hair and a gentle expression she couldn't place.

Reaching out with hesitant fingers, she skimmed the contours of the face, amazed at the smoothness of the stone. The hair actually had texture; she could feel the lines and waves that gave it movement.

Why would he create this incredible work of art featuring her, of all people? Though she'd hoped he felt something for her, he'd thrown it aside the first time she hadn't lived up to expectations. At least it felt that way. Her life had been about not making waves. But that morning, she'd gone over the top emotionally. Aiden getting angry and walking out had just confirmed her failure.

So what could he find so fascinating about her that he had to capture it in stone?

Christina started as footsteps pounded on the porch. Twisting around, she stared anxiously at the door, waiting for Aiden to walk through it and find her inside. Her stomach cramped. Had he returned? Would he be angry she'd invaded his special space?

The footsteps traveled across the boards, then stopped, giving Christina the impression that whoever it was had gone on around the side of the house.

Crossing quickly to the window, she stood to one side and cautiously leaned over to look out. She was just in time to get an impression of young men running toward the dirt track that led to mill property.

Two stood for a moment in the yard, talking, giving her a look at their faces. She recognized both: one she didn't know personally but had seen around town. The other was Raul, one of the part-time groundskeepers at Blackstone

Manor. Puzzled, she watched as they both turned away and trotted around the fence, until she lost sight of them in the woods edging the property.

A shiver worked its way down her spine as she thought of being alone inside with the men around the house. Why, she wasn't sure. She'd known Raul for over a year now. He wasn't the most personable employee, but he'd never been rude or lazy. Still, something about them upset her.

Should she wait until they were long gone before leaving? Or risk them seeing her by leaving now? What if they watched from the woods?

Turning toward the door, she decided to risk it. She'd moped around here long enough. Plus, she'd seen the guys disappear into the woods, so she should be able to get back to the house undetected.

When she was about five feet from the door, she noticed the smoke. She paused, her mind not quite understanding what the gray wisps leaking under the door meant.

As comprehension burst over her, so did a sheen of sweat. She stared, panic licking along her nerves. She shook her head to clear it, but her breath sped up no matter how much she tried to stay calm.

Numb shock cocooned her, but she was still able to acknowledge that those men had set the studio on fire. With her inside it. She didn't know how far the flames reached, but she had to find a way out. Now.

She glanced back at the only window not blocked by the air conditioner. The building wasn't that big, and by design, neither were the windows. It was a basement casement-type window, set head-high in the wall. Even if it would open all the way, she didn't think she'd fit through.

The smoke pouring in under the door grew thicker, warning her that her decision couldn't wait. She marched forward. This might not be the best option, but the door seemed to be the only exit left. She reached out, tapping the metal of the handle to test its temperature. Definitely warm, but not skin-searing yet.

Though her heart pounded and her eyes watered from the smoke, she forced herself to act. Grabbing the handle, she drew a deep breath and twisted the knob. Using the door as protection, she eased it open with slow caution.

Too late, she realized her mistake. The door swung in with a whoosh, knocking her backward. Pain exploded through her head. She tried to lift up. *What happened?* But her body refused to move. Sinking back down to the floor, she felt something trickle across her forehead.

Through the now-open doorway she could see the firelight eating away at the porch. Low on the doorway, flames inched up each side. *Move. Now.* But nothing happened. The vision before her wavered, causing nausea to rise. Closing her eyes, she tried to think.

She needed out. She couldn't move. What should she do?

Aiden jerked from automatic pilot as he caught a glimpse of a weird flickering light somewhere on the west side of Blackstone Manor. Nearing the gates, he turned in, then punched the gas. The closer he got, the more a cold grimness settled over him.

Shoving open the door so he could jump out of the truck, Aiden found himself staring at a rising plume of smoke from the vicinity of his studio. With a curse, he remembered clear as day Balcher telling him to watch out. Aiden was too careful and too familiar with studio work for this to be a result of his use of the building, and he'd had all the electrical lines checked out. Had the rival businessman decided to strike at the Blackstones a little closer to home?

Anger tightened his chest. If the man wanted to send a message, he'd sent it to the wrong person. Aiden would make sure Balcher paid for this little stunt, and paid dearly.

Rushing out of the truck, he jogged to join Jacob and the others on the lawn. "What happened?"

Jacob pointed back at the house. "I saw the flames as I passed by a window and alerted Nolen. We've called the fire department, but it will take them a bit to get this far out."

"How long?"

"At least another ten minutes," Nolen answered. "We're getting some hoses to hook up to the outdoor faucet in the well house down there, but I don't know how much good it will do. I'm sorry, Master Aiden."

"I know, Nolen." He turned his back, looking over the small group. Marie watched from a little farther away, a shawl draped over her nightgown. Nicole stood with her arm around her grandmother. Luke and the gardener, who had an apartment over the garage, came around the corner of the house dragging hoses. The only ones missing were Lily and—

"Where's Christina?"

The men looked at each other, then around the back lawn. Aiden's whole body tightened.

"I guess she didn't come out," Jacob said. "She must still be in the house."

Nolen was already shaking his head as Aiden spoke. "Have you ever known her to not be involved in something with this household?" He turned to sprint toward the cabin, adrenaline surging through his veins.

"I thought the cabin was locked," Jacob yelled from beside him as they ran.

It seemed like forever before they reached the clearing now dusky with smoke. A quick glance back showed the other men were headed their way, loaded down with hoses and buckets. Just as the heat burned a little too close, Aiden heard a faint noise. He stopped short, trying to slow his breathing so he could listen. "What is that?"

"Someone calling for help," Jacob said around his panting breaths. "She's inside."

Looking around, Aiden noticed the porch was pretty well engulfed in the flames. He wouldn't fit in through the window. But he needed in, quick. Darting around, he faced the steps to the porch.

"Aiden, don't," Jacob called, but Aiden couldn't listen. If he thought too long, it would be too late, and he couldn't leave Christina inside. That simply wasn't an option.

The fire was heaviest along the wall, less so among the new boards on the porch. Aiden closed his mind off to the sensation of heat, pulled the collar of his shirt up over his nose, and dashed across the porch, praying the boards held under his feet. He'd barely breeched the doorway before he stumbled over Christina on the floor.

Oh, Lord. Please no. His heart resumed its pounding as her head lifted slightly. "Come on, baby. Let's get out of here."

"Aiden?" she asked in a cracking voice then immediately started coughing. Lifting her up and over his shoulder, he turned back toward the door. It was hard to see for all the smoke, but it looked like someone was spraying water onto the fire. Aiden made straight for the lower flame and raced back outside, welcoming the cool shower in the midst of the blistering heat.

He cleared the stairs to find the gardener and Nolen manning the hose. Jacob and Luke helped him get Christina laid out on the grass. She continued to cough, rolling over onto her side.

That's when Aiden saw the blood.

"Get that hose over here," Jacob commanded.

They sprayed both Aiden and Christina down, making sure no lingering embers were on their clothes, then returned to their attempt to keep the fire from spreading.

Aiden wiped at the blood covering one side of Christina's face. "Luke, what does this look like to you?" he asked, knowing that his brother had first-aid training for his racing profession.

Luke shined his flashlight on Christina's face. She flinched, letting her eyes squeeze tightly shut. Her teeth started to chatter, interrupted by more coughing.

"I think it's just a cut, which isn't surprising. Head wounds bleed a lot. But there'll be paramedics with the fire trucks. Definitely want this looked at."

Aiden was grateful help was on its way. He didn't care about the studio, or his work and tools inside. Only this woman. If anything happened to her, he'd be lost for sure.

Not much later, the back lawn of Blackstone Manor was filled with vehicles and flashing lights. Three volunteer fire trucks had arrived minutes after local police officers. The ambulance, and even some county officers, were now on the scene.

Christina was being treated. She hadn't looked at him, hadn't asked for him. There was only that single time she'd called his name. That might haunt him for another twenty years or so.

Aiden had allowed the paramedics to treat the larger of his wounds, then he'd dismissed them to check out the other men. Instead of hovering, Aiden searched until he found his brother standing with the fireman in charge, two police officers in uniform and Bateman, who had on a volunteer firefighter jacket. Silence fell as he approached the group.

"Do we know what the hell happened yet?" he asked, his voice deep, harsh.

The men glanced at one another, then focused on Jacob, who nodded at one of the policemen. He introduced himself to Aiden. "From what we've been able to gather, right as the sun went down, five male individuals took it upon themselves to burn the building down. The burn patterns indicate they spread an accelerant, then lit various spots around the building."

"Five males? Do we know any of them?"

Jacob nodded. "Raul, one of the gardeners."

"So you have them in custody already?"

The policeman shook his head. "Not yet, but we've put out APBs for them. They won't get far."

Aiden looked out across the chaos of the back lawn. "If you haven't caught them, how do you know who it was?"

"Your wife was able to ID two of them—"

So much had happened, Aiden was having a hard time comprehending. "So she saw them as they set fire to the building?"

"She saw two of them clearly, and identified the gardener," the officer said. "The others she just saw running into the woods. It wasn't until she approached the door that she realized what had happened."

How terrified she must have been to know the building was on fire, yet be afraid to go out the door. Bile rose in the back of Aiden's throat, forcing him to swallow. "What was she doing in there?"

Jacob shook his head. "I'm not sure."

Guilt shot through Aiden. He should be with her. But would she want him? Another hard swallow helped him regain his equilibrium. But he wasn't sure how long it would last.

The lights surrounding them lit up Jacob's face in flashes of red and blue. Aiden clearly saw the other man's jaw tighten. "Somehow she hit her head and went down as she opened the door. I guess she thought she had no choice but to jump through the flames off the front porch."

Dizziness raced through Aiden. Though he thought he might go down, he managed to stay upright by sheer will and tightening his grasp on his brother. Clenching his jaw kept him from screaming his frustration.

Intellectually, he knew he would care about anyone who'd gotten hurt, but his emotions were ricocheting all over the place. Though they'd left things on rough footing, his week away had only confirmed his feelings for his wife. He didn't know what would happen, but in this moment, it didn't matter.

He had to be with her. Right. Now.

Jacob trailed behind as Aiden made a beeline for one of

the ambulances, where a paramedic stood talking to Marie. A second paramedic was packing up the equipment. "How is she?" Jacob asked as they approached.

Marie turned to them with worry clearly stamped in her furrowed brow and the tightness around her mouth. "Better, I think."

Aiden pushed forward for a glimpse into the interior of the vehicle. Christina lay on a gurney. The dim lighting allowed him to see her body tucked underneath a white sheet, the paleness of her skin against the tangle of her dark hair, and the oxygen mask against her mouth. Blood was still smeared in haphazard streaks along the right side of her face.

Aiden turned to the paramedic near him. "How is she, really?"

The man met his gaze head-on, reassuring Aiden somewhat. "She has lung irritation from extended smoke inhalation. We're going to take her to the hospital so they can watch her lungs for a little while. There are a couple of small burns we've treated where her clothes caught on fire. The cut on her forehead will need stitches."

Aiden's jaw tightened at the picture the other man's words sent to his brain.

"But all in all, she's very lucky."

Aiden glanced back at the woman who was his wife, whom he'd refused to contact over the last week as he'd vacillated between irritation and need. Regret pushed to the forefront of the emotions swirling through him.

"Sir, we really need to get you checked out, too."

Aiden nodded in acknowledgment, not trusting himself to speak. Another medic let them know he was ready to drive Christina to the hospital.

Aiden's first instinct was to insist on riding in the ambulance so he could be there with Christina. But she had yet to open her eyes. He wasn't sure if she was asleep or just avoiding him.

Unsure of his welcome, Aiden turned to Marie. "Could you and Nolen possibly follow them? She'll want someone with her, and I need to finish up a few things here." Not anything that he couldn't delegate to his brothers. But then again, hadn't he spent his entire life off-loading his responsibilities onto them?

Marie nodded. "I'll keep you boys up-to-date on what's happening. Until you can get there, that is."

Quite frankly, he might be the last person Christina wanted to see. No harm in letting them run the preliminary tests, so he'd have some information by the time he got down there. "Let me know the minute they tell you anything. I'll be there as soon as I've sorted out some of this mess."

The ambulance closed up. Nolen led Marie to his truck. Within minutes, they were both on the move, the ambulance siren blaring a warning to anyone who got in the way.

Aiden turned back toward the chaos of cars, people, and trampled plants that now constituted the back formal lawn. He took in the rubble that was now his studio, once the roof had caved. He couldn't imagine Christina, resourceful as she was, fighting her way out of that building. The very thought terrified him.

As Aiden stared at the activity before him—the firemen spraying the collapsed building, Luke and Nicole handing out cups of coffee and snacks, the policeman standing with his notepad, jotting down his thoughts from the interviews—a familiar sense of guilt wavered through him.

But for once, he would not let it keep him away from those he loved. Not this time. Not ever again.

Seventeen

Drawn to the woman he loved like a puppet on a string, Aiden approached her hospital bed with caution. Sitting in the chair beside her wouldn't do it. He needed to be near, to touch her and assure himself that she was okay. The doctor said they only wanted to monitor her oxygen, but the need remained.

Her body was so still. Was she sunk deep in the healing sleep she so desperately needed? Or was she pretending to sleep so she didn't have to deal with him at all?

Taking a chance, he settled on the space beside her in the bed. There was just enough room for him to sit, his thigh resting along the curve of her back as she faced the opposite wall. Testing his welcome, he lay his hand on top of her hip. Sure enough, her body jerked, though there was nowhere for her to go.

"Christina," he said, the soulful sound tinged with pain and regret.

She didn't respond, but her muscles tightened under his touch. Though he regretted the rejection, at least she knew he was here, was aware, even if she didn't like it.

"Are you all right? Is there anything I can get you?" Aiden made a sucky nursemaid, as evidenced by his inability to even set foot in his mother's room, but he had a lot to make up for here.

Christina didn't respond, but he heard a slight catch in

her breath. His eyes drifted shut, letting his senses focus solely on her, instead of the shadows from the light of the television in the far corner of the room.

"Christina, I know I screwed up, honey, and I'm sorry." He paused to see if any response came. But she seemed to curl in on herself even more than before. His hand rubbed absently along the curve of her spine. Up. Down. Savoring the feel of her delicate bones beneath his palm.

"Christina, I know I blew up the other day." He paused, searching for the right words, even though he knew he was going to screw this up big-time. "I got angry. You know more than anyone how easily I fly off the handle when I feel like I'm being manipulated, even if it's from the grave."

He thought he felt a catch in her breath. Was she crying? He didn't hear anything. The thought of her lying there, silent tears tracking down her face, stole his breath.

"I'm sorry for leaving like that."

This time her quavering breath was more distinguishable, but he plowed on while he could hold himself together enough to talk.

"I know I didn't call you this week, but I was trying to figure out how to apologize, and how to undo all the… crap…everything. In case you haven't noticed, I act before I think sometimes. When something means a lot to me, it takes a while for my head to catch up."

Aiden took comfort from the warmth of Christina next to him, and the darkness that hid his shame. So many times in his life his mistakes had hurt those he loved. Was he forever doomed to be defined by his mistakes?

He bent closer to her. "I'm so sorry, Christina. More than I can ever say. I know you can't forgive me right now and I can't prove to you how very sorry I am. But someday I will, Christina. I'll make it up to you. Someday."

Aching to feel her, he twisted around, lying down on the bed with his front curved against her back. They lay there in silence for long minutes before her body gradually relaxed into his.

Aiden couldn't sleep. He thought of the fragile woman in his arms, and how—just this once—he wanted to slay all her dragons. Never let anyone make her feel unwanted again. He only hoped she gave him the opportunity before it was too late.

Three days later, one very weary Aiden made his way into the local police station to meet with the deputies handling the arson case. He received some good news and some bad.

"We think we've rounded up everyone now, five in all, just like Christina said. The gardener was the last one, because he ran as soon as the others started getting picked up. Officers from the next county brought him in today. Would you mind confirming that this man was your employee?"

Aiden nodded.

As he stood in the viewing room, staring at the man who'd worked at the manor for a year at Nolen's last count, he wondered how someone could make such a grievous mistake.

"According to the other perpetrators," the officer said, "the basic plan was to burn the building down. They had no idea anyone was inside. They checked, since a single lamp was on, but didn't see anyone. This one—" he gestured to the gardener with a nod of his head "—was the ringleader. He riled them up, saying you didn't deserve to take over, and they would all eventually end up without a job. Trying to run you off, they claim."

Aiden was far from convinced. "Why? There was no proof of that. He had to be working for someone else." The question was, who? The man who wanted Aiden's company? A local upset over new management? Or some other unknown threat?

"We're hoping to get this guy to crack, but it doesn't look good. He's been tight, whereas the others opened up like the proverbial can of worms. But with our other boys ratting him out, it might give us some leverage to bargain for a name. It all depends."

Aiden inclined his head, watching the man through the one-way glass. Something about his eyes, cold and hard, told Aiden they would have to wield any leverage they had very carefully. This wasn't some punk running the streets or a teen led astray. According to the cop, he suspected the guy had done time in juvie, though he couldn't prove it. And he carried a look like he didn't care what happened to him. Balcher could have promised him a lot of things, including paying more if he kept his mouth shut. If the price was right, this one just might hold out.

"Did you find anything to link him to Balcher?" Aiden asked. He'd mentioned his conversation with the rival businessman the first time he'd talked with the officer.

"No. He was at a convention and received an award in front of five hundred people the night of the fire. And the gardener's phone records show no link to Balcher."

As the detective went on, Aiden felt his frustration grow. He wanted Balcher responsible because it made the most sense, and he wanted this over for Christina. She'd been shut down ever since the fire. Not just with him, but with everybody. He didn't want her worried about her safety. But Aiden had a feeling that, until they could find out who was truly behind this, none of them would be safe.

"Let me know if you find out anything."

The detective nodded. "We will. And I'd just like to say, for the record, that we do appreciate all you're doing to keep the mill going. It can't be easy uprooting your life, but it means a lot to the people of this town."

Aiden shrugged away the thanks, uncomfortable in his role as savior. "You can thank Jacob when you see him next. Having someone who's better versed in this stuff has made all the difference."

"But you will be staying, right?"

Aiden nodded slowly. "I will." *If Christina still wants me to.*

The other man nodded, and they exchanged a few pleasantries before Aiden made his way out to the car. He paused beside it, staring up into the bright sunshine under a cloudless sky. Honestly, the last thing he wanted was to go home. Back to Blackstone Manor, though the mere fact that he'd begun to think of it as home had come as a huge surprise to him.

Maybe he was growing up after all, he thought with a smirk. The place was crowded with his family now, though Luke didn't make it back as often. Still, having his brothers around both eased his own burdens and was a whole lot of fun. The camaraderie they'd shared on those visits as adults continued, even though they saw each other more now. Aiden had even been talking to a contractor about having a new studio built, along with a warehouse to move his base of operations here instead of New York.

The only fly in the ointment was Christina. Seeing her looking so calm was upsetting. That made no sense, except Aiden knew the facade was fake. And he had a feeling she was restless because she wasn't working, too. They'd hired a temporary caregiver for a couple of weeks to take over Lily's care, because Christina had been told to take it easy while her lungs and wounds healed. Aiden insisted on sleeping with Christina, using the excuse that he could listen out for Lily at night, but she kept herself stiffly on her side of the bed.

Except every morning they woke up in the same position: Aiden curled around her with their legs tangled together. She never mentioned it. Neither did he. But that was about to change.

Aiden feared if he wasn't able to break through the wall Christina had erected to protect herself, he'd lose her for good. She'd been neglected too often in the past to forget, so he'd been trying to give her time. Instead, she seemed to be slipping farther from his grasp with each passing day.

If she'd just give him a chance, they would have a future together. Right now, that's what Aiden wanted more than anything else in the world. More than his business. More than tearing up James's will.

Even more than his freedom.

Eighteen

She was crying over shoes. Christina knew she was in a pitiful state, but this was more than even she could condone. Shoes were shoes. And as Christina sat in front of her open closet, she knew she shouldn't make any decisions in this frame of mind.

Because choosing which shoes to get rid of should not make her cry.

In reality, her over-the-top emotions had nothing to do with shoes and everything to do with Aiden. He was always busy, but until today, always within reach. The problem? He treated her like a delicate figurine that would break with a simple touch.

She missed how he threw himself into everything, right or wrong. She missed arguing and the comfortableness of working together. The connection that she'd felt when they'd talked about his father. The awe she'd felt when he stood up to her father. Above all, she missed the intensity of his passion, and the feel of her soul mingling with his.

The days were torture. The nights were devastating.

They went to sleep, each on their respective sides of the bed. Some nights, lying there feeling useless and empty, Christina thought she'd give anything to have him curled against her back like he had that night in the hospital. Sure enough, by morning they would be tangled together, and her heart broke all over again. Something had to give soon because having him close but not having him for real was killing her. If she was braver, she'd ask him to stay. Why didn't she just ask?

She couldn't force herself to face any more rejection in her life.

Knowing he had left her without trying to understand her fears told her everything. All of those precious memories lay around her, shattered like broken glass. She had to escape, couldn't stand one more day moping around, wishing for things she couldn't have. But the inhabitants of Blackstone Manor had become her life; how could she possibly go?

So here she was, cleaning out her closet and crying.

As if conjured by her infernal wishing, Aiden slipped through the door. Twisting around, she stared up at him from her seat on the floor. "When did you get back?"

"Just a few minutes ago." He hesitated for a moment before speaking again. "The police now have all five of them in custody."

Christina grimaced. Just thinking about her glimpse of those men outside the cabin window gave her the shivers. She forced herself to shrug it off. "Will I have to testify?"

Aiden shook his head. "I doubt it. They have confessions out of four of them. It's a done deal. They just can't find anything that ties Balcher to the crime, and they have no other leads to who would have put them up to this. And we've found nothing more at the mill that could help."

Christina let that pass, not wanting to think about someone who was willing to destroy property to scare people away. Thugs didn't deserve her attention in any way.

To her surprise, Aiden approached with measured steps across the carpet, then knelt down beside her. She glanced up at his face but quickly looked away. He was just too beautiful for her to watch without giving away the pain she was feeling.

"Christina, what's the matter?"

Christina could feel herself close down. She wiped the tear trails from her cheeks. Experience had taught her that men didn't like messy, emotional women.

When she didn't move, he joined her on the floor. He turned her as if she were a doll so she was facing him. She couldn't quite reconcile the sophisticated, sexy businessman she knew with the casually comfortable man before her now. Instead of a T-shirt with his khakis. His hair was still tousled, but more from running his fingers through it than from gel.

Whether dressed to the nines, sweaty from sex or sitting on her bedroom floor, he was still the most attractive man she'd ever seen.

And here she was in yoga pants and a tank top, her hair pulled up in a large clip. He'd definitely gotten the raw end of their deal.

Still, he didn't move, and that waiting expression told her she better start talking. The last thing she wanted was Aiden prying into her feelings, so she chose the safest topic. "I'm struggling," she said with a shrug. "I just want things to be normal again." She gestured to her closet. "This is just so useless." *Pointless.* And it was true. Having no real purpose to her days gave her no reason to get up, no reason to do anything. Too much time to think, to mope. To feel unwanted and unneeded.

"You know we just want you to be able to heal, right?"

"Yes, Aiden. I know. But I'm fine." *I need to get back to work.*

"You don't act fine."

A quick peek from beneath her eyelashes showed that same searching expression in his eyes that had been there for a week. She didn't want to be a puzzle he had to figure out. She wanted to be a partner. In a burst of clarity, she realized he was right. She wasn't acting fine. She was moping around, hoping someone would fix all the problems, instead of taking charge.

When had waiting for someone else to make the first move done her any good? The only times she'd been happy in her life had been when she stepped up to the plate, taken on the challenge of doing what fulfilled her. Time to make something happen instead of waiting for it to happen. But what was the right step?

"I'm more than ready to take care of Lily again." That much she knew for sure. "I can't lie around here feeling useless while someone else does my job."

"Useless?" The disbelief on his face was hard to understand. But he wasted no time enlightening her. "Christina, you go out of your way to help everyone—this town, Nolen, Marie, Nicole. You sacrificed yourself to keep Lily safe—"

"Stop." She jerked to her feet. "Don't do that."

He stood, stalking closer. "Christina—"

"No." She could feel the trembling start along her nerves, fingertips to shoulders, toes to tummy. Needing to move, she paced past him. Soon she'd be an allover mess, but she had to get this out. "I didn't sacrifice myself for Lily. I love her, but I volunteered to marry you because of guilt. I *owe* Lily."

That stopped him cold. His voice, when he spoke, was softer than she expected. "What are you talking about?"

She almost wished she was facing the angry Aiden. This would be so much easier if he wasn't being so nice. "I caused her accident," she whispered.

Aiden shook his head. "No. She was coming home—"

"Because of me. You'd told her to stay an extra day to wait out the weather. But I'd gotten sick. Really bad appendicitis. I was in the hospital after having my appendix removed. Marie called Lily, told her my mother had left me there alone. Heck, she barely even stayed long enough for me to get out of recovery."

She swallowed hard, her stomach churning at the memories. "Lily came home in spite of the weather to be with me. So I wouldn't be alone. I didn't find out about the accident until I was released from the hospital."

"Oh, my God, Christina." Aiden's voice rose. He stalked forward, hands settling on her upper arms to give her a little shake. "Don't you know Lily would never feel that way? She would never blame you for what was very much an accident."

"But I blame myself. Just like I blame myself for you having to come back here, to stay here. You want to be in New York, I understand that. But instead, you're here, with me."

"That is not your fault. That's James's doing. He put us in this situation...."

"But I want you to stay."

The silence that filled the room drowned out the pounding of her heart. Had she really just said that out loud? Fear kept her from looking at him for a reaction. There was no going back now.

"You are only here because you have to be, Aiden, but I want you with me. Permanently." *I'll make it up to you.* His words from the hospital haunted her, but she had to take a risk. Could she really do this?

A hard swallow helped her continue. "I love you. Whether you're here or in New York, I will love you. But I'd much rather you be here. I'm sorry if that makes me a clingy, desperate woman. I don't want you to have to choose between being tied to a place you hate just because you slept with me, and going back to the life you love. I just...want you."

"Who says I have to choose?"

Surprise shot along her nerves.

"Christina, I've been waiting a week for you to reach for me. To need me. But you never did. I thought I made